GHOST GAME

NIGEL HINTON

NON-FICTION SECTION BY CHRISTOPHER EDGE

www.pearsonschoolsandfecolleges.co.uk

✓ Free online support
✓ Useful weblinks
✓ 24 hour online ordering

0845 630 33 33

Part of Pearson

Heinemann is an imprint of Pearson Education Limited, Edinburgh Gate, Harlow, Essex, CM20 2JE.

www.pearsonschoolsandfecolleges.co.uk

Heinemann is a registered trademark of Pearson Education Limited

Text © Nigel Hinton 2011
Non-fiction text © Christopher Edge 2011
Typeset by Kamae Design
Cover design by Wooden Ark Studios
Cover photo © Corbis

The rights of Nigel Hinton and Christopher Edge to be identified as authors of this work have been asserted by them in accordance with the Copyright, Designs and Patents Act 1988.

First published 2011

14 13 12 11 10
10 9 8 7 6 5 4 3 2 1

British Library Cataloguing in Publication Data
A catalogue record for this book is available from the British Library

ISBN 978 0 435 04595 1

Printed at Henry Ling, UK

Acknowledgements

We would like to thank the following schools and students for their invaluable help in the development and trialling of this book:

Queensbridge School, Birmingham: Farhan Akmal, Farees Almatari, Junaid Asif, Chloe Bartlett, Shane Bevan, Tyler Blair-Thompson, Shahid Farooq, Danial Hussain, Umayr Hussain, Arbaz Mohammed Khan, Kadeem Khan, Umer Khan, Ihtishaam Majid, Arslan Mehmood, Sophie Pinnegar, Aaron Reatus, Jamie-Lee Smith, Roche Smith, Abdalla Suleiman, Imran Uddin, Saqib Ul-Hassan, Chulothe Urooj, Keiran Von-Breen, Nikolas Watkins, Oliver Watkins, Grace Williams, Raakib Zaman. **Acle High School, Norwich**: Mustafa Afsar, Mohammed Akmal Ali, Nassar Ayaz, Azharudeen Basheer Ahmed, Andre Christian, Jordan Easie, Antoinette Grant, Kia Greaves, Conor Handel, Waseem Hanif, Kabeer Javed, Zeshan Javed, Abel Johnson, Selina King, Ismaeel Muhammed Majid, Aziz Rehman and Abdul Wahid.

To Joey Lager

Watching you play video games inspired this story.

CONTENTS

Non-fiction:

CHAPTER ONE

'Number thirteen?' Danny said, looking up at the dark old house. 'You're kidding. I don't want to live there.'

'Why?' his dad asked.

'Hello? Thirteen! It's bad luck, Dad.'

'Oh come on, Daniel – you don't believe in stupid superstitions.'

He was being serious – he only called him Daniel when he was serious – but Danny didn't care. 'Everyone knows – thirteen's unlucky,' he said.

'Look, it's only for a couple of months until we can buy our own place. And the rent's dirt cheap – half the price of the others they offered me.'

'No wonder – look at it. It's a dump: a dark, creepy dump.'

'Oh come on, Danny, it's just an ordinary house.' His dad smiled and then a shadow passed across his face as he added, 'Anyway, we've had our share of bad luck.'

He was right. The worst had already happened. Mum and Adam dead in a train crash. Things couldn't get any worse than that, could they?

Oh yes, they could, said a small voice at the back of Danny's brain. But he ignored it and got out of the car and followed his dad up the path.

They could get much worse, the voice went on as his dad opened the door and they walked into the house.

The long, gloomy hallway was painted dark brown, the kitchen was painted dark brown, the dining room was painted dark brown and the front room had dark and light brown striped wallpaper. Even the carpets and the long curtains against the windows were brown.

'The house is Victorian,' his dad explained. 'The owner must think the Victorians' favourite colour was brown.'

The only different colours came from a tall stained-glass window halfway up the wide staircase. It showed a sad-looking shepherd near some dark mountains. The sun was setting – just two rays of light beamed up from behind the mountains – and the shepherd was holding up a lantern to help him search for his sheep, which were grazing under some trees.

The colours – dark blue, green, red, yellow and grey – glowed from the daylight outside, but there was something creepy about the picture, as if a pack of wolves was lurking just out of sight, waiting to kill.

'Original Victorian?' Danny joked.

'Probably.'

'Now, I wonder what colour the bedrooms are? Brown, maybe,' he said and was glad to hear Dad laugh. He didn't do much laughing nowadays. And Danny suddenly decided that he wasn't going to complain any more. All right, he didn't like the house, but it was only for a short time and Dad didn't need any more worries or problems.

When they got upstairs and found that the four bedrooms were painted dark green, Danny managed to get another chuckle out of him by saying, 'They must have run out of brown!'

Dad let him have first choice of the bedrooms and he picked the one that overlooked the back garden.

'OK, I'll have the front one. I can use the little one next to it as an office. And this one can be Adam's –' Dad stopped and a flush started up his throat as they both looked at each other. 'God, what am I –'

He shook his head and there was a long silence. His eyes flicked towards the doorway of the bedroom again as if he was hoping to see Adam come running out of the room. And Danny felt the same. He closed his eyes and tried to picture his young brother leaping out with a big cry of 'BOO!' to try to scare him like he used to. He tried to see those laughing eyes and that cheeky grin. He imagined with all his might, as if he could make it happen just by wanting it enough.

Then they both jumped as the doorbell rang.

'Neighbour come to say hello?' Dad said.

'I'll go,' Danny said, and ran down the stairs. He opened the door.

No one was there.

Kids playing tricks? He looked along the street. It was empty.

He went back inside and closed the door. He had just started up the stairs when the bell rang again. He went back to the door and opened it.

No one.

For a moment he felt a faint push on his chest as if something was trying to get past him and into the house. The pressure stopped but a chill swept up his back and he slammed the door shut.

When he got upstairs Dad was still standing looking at the bedroom door, lost in his thoughts.

'It was nobody,' Danny said. He wanted to say something about what had happened at the door but Dad's face suddenly crumpled with sorrow.

'Oh, Danny, I miss them so much. Mum. And Adam – we were so close.'

He nodded. Dad and Adam had both liked doing the same things – fishing, basketball, flying model planes. After the train accident Danny had actually tried to replace his younger brother by pretending to be interested in the same things. He'd even missed playing in a couple of football matches to go fishing with Dad. It had felt really weird to hold Adam's fishing rod and to try to say things that Adam might have said. And it hadn't worked. After the second time Dad had said it was just too painful and he didn't want to go any more.

Danny had been a bit hurt, but then he had realised that he didn't want Dad to try to replace Mum. Mum was Mum and could never be replaced. So he had stopped trying to be Adam and had concentrated on being Danny: the Danny that Dad loved and needed.

'Oh well,' Dad said after a moment. 'Better unpack.'

It took Danny ages to take his clothes out of his suitcase and put them in his cupboard but he was quicker than Dad. He still had most of his things piled up on his bed when Danny went to see how he was getting on.

'I'm useless!' he said. 'Your mum would have done this in half the time. She always said I'd be lost without her – and she was right.'

'I'll help,' Danny said, and half an hour later everything was tidily arranged.

'Thanks, mate,' Dad said. 'Tell you what, let's eat out. First evening in our new town – let's celebrate with a pizza. Or whatever – you choose.'

'Pizza's good,' he said.

They drove around town and ended up in a pizzeria in the Pines Shopping Centre. Danny looked out of the window at all the young people walking up and down the mall and wondered if any of them would be in his class when he went to the new school.

Had it been a good idea to move away from their old house and their old lives? Danny wasn't sure. Dad said they both needed to start again, needed a new challenge – something to stop them thinking about Mum and Adam all the time. He was probably right, but Danny already missed his old friends and was worried about having to make new ones.

He was tired when they got back to 13 Leylyne Road so he decided to go to bed. As he brushed his teeth he glanced into the bathroom mirror. A face was looking back at him. A face so pale that he could hardly see it.

But it wasn't his face.

He dropped the toothbrush in shock.

The face faded and was gone. There was just his reflection. It must have been a trick of the light, or something wrong with the mirror. It was old – probably original Victorian. Ha ha.

Yes, it was the same old face looking back at him. Nice brown eyes. Stupid, sticky-out ears. Nose a bit crooked from when he broke it in a football game. Mum always said his nose made him look cool and tough. Adam used to say it made him look like a freak. That was Adam – always ready with a sarcastic comment, but usually right.

He switched the bedroom light off and groped his way across the room in the darkness. He stubbed his toe on a chair and decided he would have to fix up a bedside light. He found the bed and slipped in between the sheets. The mattress was hard.

He turned on his side, trying to get comfortable. Then the bedroom door opened and closed quickly.

'Dad?' he asked, raising his head.

No answer.

'Dad?'

No answer.

He sat up with his heart pounding quickly as he heard a noise near the door. Whoever had opened it, had come inside and was standing there in the dark.

'Who's there?'

There was a long pause, then his skin crawled with terror as he felt the bed move slightly. Against the thin line of light under the door he could see a dim shape. He reached out his hands but there was only emptiness.

The shape moved and drifted away towards the wall, merging with the darkness until he couldn't see it any more.

He kept very still and after a moment he was sure he could hear soft breathing from across the room. Then it faded and he allowed himself to move again.

He jumped from the bed and ran towards the door. He scrambled for the switch. The light flashed on, blinding him briefly. But when he looked towards where the figure had been, there was nobody there.

There was nobody anywhere.

The room was empty.

CHAPTER TWO

Two days later Dad started his new job. Danny stayed at 13 Leylyne Road, wishing that they hadn't arranged for him to have an extra week to settle in before he started at the new school.

It was the first time he had been alone in the house and he couldn't help noticing how many little noises there were. The wooden stairs squeaked as if someone was stepping on them. Floorboards creaked above him. Something rattled against a window. Stupid to be scared, of course. They were just ordinary noises. All houses had them. But he couldn't stop a shiver running across his shoulders.

Was it cold in here? The phrase 'As cold as the grave' came into his mind and he shivered again.

He went out into the back garden. The late summer sunshine was really hot, which made it even stranger that the house was so cold.

He was lying on the grass soaking up the sun's warmth when a beautiful black cat leaped down from the tall fence next door. Danny held out his hand and wiggled his fingers but the cat just raised its glossy black tail and stared at him with its green eyes.

'Come on, I'm not going to hurt you,' Danny said and leaned forward.

The cat arched its back, opened its mouth and hissed. Its pointed teeth looked razor sharp.

'Whoa!' he said, snatching his hand back. 'That's not very friendly.'

'Midnight? Midnight?' a voice called from the other side of the fence.

The cat turned its head towards the sound, then scooted along the fence and climbed up into a thick bush at the end of the garden. It disappeared from sight as if hiding from its owner.

'Midnight? Where are you? Come to Mummy,' the voice called again.

Danny got up and went over to the fence. He stood on one of the struts and peered over the top. An old lady was standing on the patio. Her white hair was so thin that her pink scalp showed through.

'Are you looking for your cat?' Danny asked, and the old lady jumped in shock. 'He's hiding in a bush over here. He's beautiful. Is it a he or a she?'

The lady backed through the patio doors, closed them, and drew the curtains to hide herself from view.

'Friendly cat, friendly owner!' Danny muttered as he got down from the fence.

A moment later the cat poked its head out of the bush to check that its mistress had gone then it jumped back into its own garden.

The next day Danny was alone in the back garden again when a voice called from next door, 'You. Young man.'

'Do you mean me?' he asked, peering over the fence.

The old lady was standing on the patio again. She still seemed nervous when she saw Danny but she nodded at the black cat in her arms. 'Would you like to meet Midnight? Come round to the front and I'll let you in.'

Later, Danny couldn't understand why Miss White had invited him in because she didn't seem to want to talk. She just sat with Midnight on her lap and stared out of the window while Danny asked questions and got very short answers. Finally, he ran out of things to say. There was a long silence and he looked at the strange painting on the wall. It showed a blue lion standing next to a green unicorn. Above the two animals there was a hand with an eye in its palm, and above that a rainbow. It was one of the ugliest paintings he had ever seen. On the small table under the painting, two incense sticks were burning and the smoke curled upwards, filling the room with a sweet smell.

Danny was about to tell Miss White that he would have to go when she spoke, 'I've got the Sight, you know.'

'Sorry?'

'The Sight. I can see things other people can't. It's a gift from God. A gift … and a curse.'

Danny didn't know what to say and he wished he'd left. The room had suddenly become very stuffy, the incense was making him feel sick, and the old lady was starting to scare him.

'There's sadness in your life, isn't there?' Miss White whispered, raising goose pimples on Danny's skin.

'Yes,' he heard himself say.

'I knew it. I can see it all round you. Deep, deep sadness. Something bad happened. Yes?'

Danny nodded, his throat too choked to speak. Tears filled his eyes and he suddenly wanted to tell this old lady everything. He hardly knew her but there was something about her that made Danny want to pour out all the pain he'd been keeping inside, all the pain he'd tried to hide from everyone.

He wanted to cry and tell her how much he missed Adam. But most of all, how much he missed Mum and how he wanted to hug her and talk to her like he used to. Maybe if he told Miss White he would feel better.

But he stopped himself and said he had to go. Miss White smiled and lifted her hand in a farewell wave. As soon as he got out of the house he breathed deeply, letting the fresh air wash away the stuffy sweetness of Miss White's room.

When he told his dad about the visit to their neighbour he said, 'She sounds like a nutter. The Sight! The silly old biddy's just trying to make herself seem important.'

Yes, she probably was a silly old biddy, but during the evening Danny couldn't stop thinking about Miss White. Dad went to bed early so Danny was alone when a horror film came on TV. Usually he loved scary movies but this one was about a man who could see bad things that were going to happen to people – a bit like Miss White with the Sight. The film started to give him the creeps and he turned it off after ten minutes.

The scary feeling got worse as he started up the stairs. Dad had turned off the landing light, and the higher he climbed the darker it became. By the time he got to his room and put his light on, his nerves were tingling. He'd never been scared like this in their *old* house.

It was stupid. Stupid. He kept telling himself there was nothing to be frightened of, but he couldn't make the fear go away.

He sat at his desk and opened his sketchbook. Drawing always helped him to forget things and get him in the mood for sleep. He did a picture of the things on his desk and then he started drawing a face. It wasn't meant to be anyone – just a general face – but the more he worked at it, the more he realised it was beginning to look exactly like Adam. He deliberately changed it, adding a moustache, long hair and an earring. But even then, the eyes staring back at him from the paper – they were Adam's eyes. He added dark glasses to cover them up. He drew a scar across the cheek. Now it didn't look anything like Adam, but it was ugly and horrible. Like a killer's face.

He put the pencils back in his pencil case and closed it, then shut the sketchbook. It had worked – drawing had made him tired. When he got into bed he fell asleep quickly.

The next morning he was about to go down for breakfast when he glanced at his desk and saw that the pencil case and sketchbook were open. All his pens and pencils were lying in a line next to the drawing of that ugly face.

There was a mark on the paper under the face as if someone had tried to write something. He peered at it closely. What was is it? It looked like the letter D.

D for …? D for Danny? D for … danger?

Daylight was pouring through his window and he could hear his dad downstairs cooking breakfast and listening to the radio. It was an ordinary morning – but the hairs on his arms were rising in fear. Something was wrong with this house. Very wrong.

CHAPTER THREE

As soon as Dad left for work, Danny knew that he would only get scared if he stayed in the house so he went next door and rang Miss White's bell.

This time he didn't bother to ask any questions, just sat waiting until the old lady was ready to talk. The grandfather clock in the corner ticked away the seconds and Danny found himself counting them, dividing them into minutes. He had reached five minutes and eight seconds when Miss White sighed.

'You're curious about the Sight,' she said. She closed her eyes and rolled her head from side to side against the back of the tall armchair as if she was struggling against something. 'It frightened me when it started. I was about your age when I realised I could see things that other people couldn't. I didn't understand it and I tried to hide it. I hated it – seeing things I didn't want to see.'

'Like what?' Danny asked.

'The dead.'

Miss White's pale blue eyes shot open wide and a chill fell on Danny.

'And the dying,' Miss White went on. 'I can look at someone and know that Death is sitting on their shoulders.'

Danny shivered as the old lady's eyes bored into him.

'Me?' he asked.

'You?' Miss White said, her eyes widening. 'No. The blood beats strongly in you.'

Danny felt pleased, but he couldn't help remembering his dad's comment: 'The silly old biddy's trying to make herself seem important.'

'When you say you see the dead,' Danny said, 'do you mean like ghosts?'

Miss White nodded. 'I prefer to call them spirits.'

'Are they real then?'

'You know they are. That's why you're interested in them,' the old lady said. She leaned forward and grasped Danny's hand. 'Your mother … she's … not with you?'

Once again Danny felt tears come into his eyes and Miss White's hand tightened round his.

'She's … passed away, hasn't she? Yes, I knew it.'

The old lady closed her eyes and tilted her head to one side, as if she was listening to something.

'Your mother was Welsh, wasn't she?'

'Sort of. Her parents were English but they moved to Wales when she was a baby so she was brought up there. How did you know?'

'I know many things. I know you're sad. But you shouldn't be. Your mother's at peace. She's happy. Resting in peace.'

'How do you –' Danny began, then stopped as Miss White put her finger to her lips and smiled.

'No questions. I'm tired – it wears me out to be in touch with the Other Side. You just go on home and think about what I've told you.'

Dad got angry that evening when Danny told him about the conversation. He said that Miss White was worse than a silly old biddy – she was a wicked, lying witch who was trying to take advantage of other people's grief.

'But she knew Mum was dead.' Danny said.

'Big deal! She notices that there isn't a woman around so she knows either we've split up or Mum's dead. She watches you closely, asks a few clever little questions to give her a clue, and then amazes you by apparently getting a message from "the Other Side". I'll give her a message round the other side of her head if she keeps filling you up with this rubbish.'

'But she knew Mum was Welsh. How could she know that?'

'Easy. Whenever you say your name you always give it a little Welsh accent, the way Mum used to. The old witch puts two and two together and has a lucky guess. Honestly, Dan, I can't stop you seeing this old bat, but you shouldn't listen to all her nonsense – you'll just get hurt.'

Dad poured a huge glass of whisky and gulped half of it. He'd already got through nearly a whole bottle of wine with his meal so Danny decided to say goodnight and go up to his room. He hated it when Dad drank too much. It seemed to happen a lot nowadays.

That night he woke up and peered at his alarm clock. 12.45. He was about to slip back into sleep when he heard a noise. He lifted his head from the pillow and listened. There was a scraping sound as if something was being dragged across the floor, then a tapping on the wall. It came from the next room.

His skin prickled with fear and his heart began to pound. Somebody was in the empty bedroom. The noise stopped. He lay for a while, straining to hear more, but there was silence and he gradually started to calm down.

It was stupid to be scared. All that talk about ghosts with Miss White had made him nervous. So what had made the noise? Dad maybe. But what would he be doing at this time of night? Moving furniture? Maybe he had got through even more whisky and was drunk? Well, get up and check.

He started to slide out of bed, then he got back in and pulled the duvet over himself. Why wasn't he going to check? Because he didn't believe it was his dad. Dad was asleep – he had heard him come up to bed. So who was it?

What was it? He didn't know and he didn't want to know. He pulled the duvet up over his head and blocked his ears so that he wouldn't hear anything.

Sleep was a long time coming.

CHAPTER FOUR

Danny knew his dad would say it was nonsense if he tried to tell him how he felt about 13 Leylyne Road, so he kept quiet. But at the weekend, when Dad went house-hunting, he went with him, hoping they would find a new house quickly. They saw dozens of places but nothing they really liked.

'There's no rush,' Dad said. 'We're bound to find something by Christmas.'

Christmas! The thought of having to go on living in that spooky house until then …

On Monday, Danny left the house a few minutes after Dad went to work. He walked to the local park and sat watching a woman pushing her little girl on a swing. He couldn't help thinking about Mum. Maybe she had pushed him on a swing like that when he was young. As he walked towards the street a thought hit him: suppose Dad met someone else and fell in love?

What would that be like? He didn't like the idea of someone trying to replace his mum. But on the other hand he wanted Dad to be happy. It wasn't fair to expect him to spend the rest of his life alone, feeling sad and missing Mum.

He was so caught up in the idea that, before he knew where he was, he found himself turning in to Leylyne Road. He could see the high slate roof of number thirteen rising above the trees ahead of him. He didn't want to go in to that silent, empty house just yet. He looked at number eleven and wondered about visiting Miss White – he hadn't seen her for nearly a week. He hesitated because he didn't fancy listening to more stuff about ghosts and the Sight, but then he started up his path anyway. He needed company and perhaps he could steer the old lady away from talking about supernatural things.

Miss White burst into a smile when she opened the door and she immediately asked him in. She made some tea and they sat in the living room. There was no incense burning this time and Miss White seemed much less weird than before. She started talking about Midnight, then brought out a photo album and showed him pictures of other cats she had owned. She told some funny stories about their antics and Danny was glad he'd decided to come. This was what he needed: a light-hearted chat with a friendly, normal neighbour.

Then, suddenly, the whole mood changed when Danny happened to say that one of the cats looked a bit like a tiger.

Miss White closed the album and her face took on a serious look as she leaned forward and said, 'That's because cats are still in touch with their wild natures. It's what gives them their magical powers.'

Danny tried to think of something to change the subject but Miss White went on, her voice becoming slower and dreamier as she described how healers and witches and wizards always had cats as their closest companions.

'There are thousands of years of wisdom in cats,' the old lady said, stroking Midnight. 'People say they've got nine lives but they've got far more than that. In one of his other lives Midnight belonged to one of the pharaohs in ancient Egypt, didn't you, my precious? He's got royal blood.'

The idea seemed ridiculous to Danny but the way the black cat was staring at him certainly made him look noble and proud.

'I don't think he likes me much,' he said.

'He's just frightened of where you live,' Miss White said.

'Why?'

'Cats are sensitive, my dear. They can feel things – they pick up vibrations. Midnight can feel the power of the house.'

Danny didn't want to hear this. He didn't want to know about the power of the house. He wanted to get up and leave, but he couldn't stop himself from asking, 'What power?'

'People never stay there long.'

'Why?'

'Do you really want to know?'

Danny didn't want to know. But he *had* to know. He nodded.

'Certain places act like a magnet. They attract spirits,' Miss White said.

21

'Our house is a magnet?' Danny asked.

'Yes. The rent is cheap, isn't it?'

Danny nodded – his dad had said that it was half the price of the other places they'd seen.

'That's because they can't get anyone to stay there. And you know why – you've started to feel it already, I can see it in your eyes. That house has the power to attract the dead. It's haunted.'

She's just a silly old biddy, Danny kept thinking as he walked away from Miss White's house at the end of the morning. 'A silly old biddy,' he repeated to himself as he put the key in the door of number thirteen. 'A silly old biddy,' he told himself again as he stepped inside.

He closed the front door and stood in the cold hallway. Silence. Dust was floating in the coloured light from the stained-glass window. It swirled and flowed into different shapes and Danny watched it and told himself that a silly old biddy like Miss White would look at the swirling dust and say it was a magic sign or a ghost. A silly old biddy just took ordinary, natural things and tried to make them special and supernatural.

And yet … And yet … Even before he'd met Miss White, he had felt there was something strange about this house. From the very first day. It was more than the stupid superstition about the number thirteen. Much more. The moment he'd stepped foot in the house he had felt something. And not something good. Something bad.

There was a creaking noise and Danny's eyes shot back to the staircase. The dust was swirling faster now in the coloured light. As if there was a draught. As if someone had just walked up the stairs and sent the dust whirling round and round.

'Stop it!' he cried out loud. He was only telling himself to stop thinking scary thoughts, but it was as if the dust had heard him. It stopped swirling and began to float down towards the stair carpet.

Danny took a pace back, opened the front door, and went back outside. He closed the door and sat on the top step to calm the rapid beating of his heart. Out here in the open air with the sun warming his face, he could hardly believe how stupid he'd been – to be scared by dust and a creaking noise. Because that's all it was. Ordinary, everyday things. He was getting as bad as Miss White.

He waited for a while then went back inside. And this time he didn't stand listening to the silence or staring at the dust, he went straight into the kitchen, turned the radio on and let the music cheer him up while he made a cheese sandwich for lunch.

He spent most of the afternoon preparing a chilli con carne for their evening meal. After Mum had died Dad had said that they would go on having proper meals. 'A meal cooked by one of us. And we eat at a table, talking to each other, the way we've always done. No eating in front of the TV. Mum would have hated that.' So Danny had started to learn to cook. He had dug out Mum's old cookery books and was making his way slowly through the recipes.

By the time he'd finished cooking, all his stupid fears had gone away and he didn't even bother to leave the music on when he went to his room. He lost track of time, chatting on the computer to his mates from his old school, and he was surprised when he heard his dad come home and call up to him.

They sat at the kitchen table later, eating the chilli, and Dad told him about his new job and the people he was working with. Danny noticed that Dad drank nearly a whole bottle of wine during the meal and then had a big glass of whisky when they began to watch TV. He finished the whisky quickly and fell asleep just as a film started. He woke up halfway through the film and said he was going to bed but Danny stayed to watch to the end.

The whole evening had gone by without a single thought about what Miss White had said about the house, but it all came crashing back when he went up to his room. As he opened the door to his bedroom he looked back along the landing and saw a shape at the top of the stairs.

His heart jolted with shock, and ice and fire ran through his body.

It looked like a boy.

Danny ran into his room and slammed the door shut. His heart was pounding fast. His legs felt weak and he leaned against the door to stop himself falling.

BANG! BANG!

The knocking on the door shook his whole body. But he rammed his shoulder hard against the door to stop him coming in.

Him?

The boy.

The door handle rattled.

'Danny? Danny?' Dad's voice.

He fumbled with the door and opened it. Dad was standing there in his pyjamas.

'You OK?' Dad asked, bleary-eyed. 'I heard you slam the door and I thought something must have happened.'

Danny wanted to tell him, but he couldn't. 'Sorry – the door just slammed,' he said.

Dad looked at him strangely but then shrugged his shoulders. 'OK. See you in the morning. Sleep well.'

Sleep well. Danny didn't know if he would ever be able to sleep well in this house.

CHAPTER FIVE

Danny sat there, wishing he hadn't come back to talk to Miss White again, but he wanted to know, and needed to know. 'You said my mum was happy – that she was at peace. How do you know that?' he asked

'God has given me the gift of spirit contact,' the old lady said. 'When I was talking to you about her, I could feel her close to me and there was peace and contentment all around her.'

Danny was pleased that Mum was happy and at ease but he couldn't stop himself sulkily asking, 'Doesn't she miss us?'

Miss White smiled. 'Why should she? She's closer to you now than when she was alive. She knows everything about you – what you think, what you feel. She's part of you.'

Tears welled up in Danny's eyes at the thought of his mum there beside him and part of him.

Miss White gently lifted Midnight off her lap and put him on the floor. The cat stepped towards him and rubbed itself against his legs before it wandered off. Danny turned his head, pretending to be interested in where the cat was going so that he could blink the tears away. Midnight sat down in a pool of sunlight near the window and raised his paw and licked it. He felt Miss White take his hands and rub them gently so he turned back to face her.

'You loved your mother a lot, didn't you?'

Danny nodded.

'Well then, you should be happy, because she's not suffering any more.'

'What do you mean?'

'Illness and everything,' Miss White said.

'She wasn't ill.'

Miss White closed her eyes, 'But she died …'

'It was a train crash,' Danny said.

'Yes, yes, I know. That's why I said she died without suffering illness. It was a blessing.'

Miss White turned her head and screwed her eyes up as if she was in pain or as if she was trying to listen to something far away.

'What?' she asked. 'I'm sorry – I don't get that.' Her pale blue eyes opened and looked directly at Danny. 'She's trying to tell me about the crash but I can't make sense of it. It wasn't near here, was it?'

'No, it was in Wales. Mum and my brother were going to visit my grandfather when the train hit a goods train. They were in the first coach and …' Danny's throat tightened – he couldn't go on.

'Yes, yes, that's it,' Miss White said, squeezing Danny's hands. 'It was a terrible shock but your mother says that you've got to be brave and let her go now.'

'I don't want to forget her.'

'Oh, dear child, you won't forget her. She'll always be in your heart and she'll always be there to take care of you. But she says you've got to move on. She wants to watch you growing and getting on with your life. She says you're going to a new school soon, is that right? Well, she wants you to work hard and do well … or else!'

Danny felt calm and relaxed after the talk with Miss White and number thirteen seemed warmer and friendlier when he got indoors. It was wonderful to think that Mum was there with him, watching him, and taking care of him. The sun was shining through the stained-glass window and its coloured light glowed all around him as he walked upstairs. It felt as if his mum was giving him a warm hug.

Even his dad noticed and asked what had happened to make him seem so happy. He just shrugged and smiled – he didn't want to tell Dad because he'd only make some cutting remark about Miss White.

He woke up in the night, feeling very cold. He wrapped the duvet round himself. He was drifting off to sleep again when he heard something like a whisper.

There it was again – a voice was whispering.

He strained to hear what it was saying.

What was it?

The voice came louder and a chill swept through him.

One word shivered out of the darkness – 'Danny.'

He pulled his duvet up over his head and blocked his ears. He didn't want to hear whispers in the dark.

CHAPTER SIX

On Friday evening Dad brought home a DVD he'd rented. They usually watched a film at the end of the week and he told Danny that he'd chosen this one because he and Mum had seen it on their first date.

Danny tried to imagine his parents going to the cinema before he was born – had they sat in the back row and held hands and kissed? It would be fun to watch the film they'd seen all those years ago.

But as soon as the DVD started, Dad started drinking whisky. Fast. In twenty minutes he drank four large glasses. Danny didn't like to see him gulping the drinks with no pleasure – as if all he wanted to do was to get drunk. And he didn't like the film either. It all took place in dark rooms and it was terribly sad: a man and a woman were splitting up because they couldn't bear to live together after their son was killed.

Danny felt a kind of gloom creeping into his body. Then the gloom sparked into anger towards his dad. Why was he drinking so much? And why would he want to watch a miserable film about death and losing people? Was he trying to make him depressed? He could feel his anger build until he wanted to scream. He had to stop the film.

Stop it!

At that moment, the lights went off and the TV went dark.

Danny jolted with shock. Had he done that?

'Damn,' his dad said, getting up and stumbling towards the window to look through the curtains. 'The lights are on over the road – something must have tripped our fuse. The fuse box is in the cellar and we haven't got a torch or any candles.'

Danny stood in the hall, listening to Dad swearing as he groped his way down to the cellar in the dark.

'God, it's as cold as the grave down here!' Dad called. 'Urgghhh, cobwebs too – got one all over my face.'

A movement caught Danny's eye and he saw a point of green light move slowly across the hall and rise above the staircase. It grew larger, glowing and changing shape, floating like one of the bubbles in a lava lamp. And now another one suddenly flicked on. And then a third. A fourth. Four bubbles of light. They twisted round and round, spinning faster, so that they left streaks of light as they moved.

And now the cold hit him. His breath was steaming and the air was so icy that it seemed to clamp to his skin. The lights stopped moving and, as they hung there, Danny had the horrible feeling that they were eyes, looking at him.

He stepped back and bumped into the wall. The lights glowed brighter for an instant as if they had noticed his movement, as if they'd seen that he was trapped. They started coming towards him.

'Dad!' he tried to shout, but the word came out as a whisper as if the air had frozen his throat.

The lights were round him now: one to his left, one to his right and the other two directly in front of him. He was surrounded. They stopped moving and he felt as if they were watching him, examining him.

'Dad!' This time his voice was louder. 'Dad, quick!'

'What?'

'Quick!' Danny called.

'Hold on a bit. Ah, here it is.'

Suddenly, the light flashed on and the sound of the TV burst from the front room. The four glowing bubbles disappeared, lost in the brightness. The temperature went back to normal. It all happened so fast that Danny felt stunned. Dark to light. Cold to warm. The menace gone.

'It was the main switch – Lord knows what tripped it,' his dad said as he walked out of the cellar door, dragging his fingers through his hair. 'Have I still got cobwebs on me? I walked through dozens of them in the dark.'

Danny took a quick look as Dad bowed his head. 'No, they've gone.'

'Good.'

'Dad …'

He tried to explain about the strange lights but it was hard. It all seemed like a dream. Or a nightmare. Real and terrifying one minute and then gone when you woke up.

'Must have been car headlights shining through the window,' Dad said.

'It wasn't anything like headlights!'

'So what was it?'

'I don't know. Something weird, like supernatural.'

'Come on, Dan, it must have been headlights.'

'What about the cold? It was freezing.'

'Must have been a draught from the cellar – it was icy down there.'

'Oh, you don't believe in anything. You try to make everything … normal. Ordinary.'

'That's because they are, Dan. Things *are* normal. Things *are* ordinary.'

'No, they're not! Not all the time. There are things … Oh, you just don't get it!'

He couldn't tell him what Miss White had said, couldn't tell him that this house was a magnet for ghosts. He almost didn't believe it himself. It was all mixed up. One moment it seemed so real and the next it slipped away. And it made him angry that Dad didn't understand. And he wanted Mum back – she'd always understood.

'Anyway, I don't want to watch that film – I hate it! And you're drunk!' he blurted out, hoping to hurt him, and seeing in his eyes that he had.

Dad shrugged and went back to the front room.

Danny went upstairs and turned on his computer to chat to his friends, but no one was online. Friday evening – they were probably all out together enjoying themselves. He went to bed and lay there, trying to recapture the good feeling of Mum being around him, and part of him. But it didn't work. Mum seemed a long way away.

He could hear the distant sound of the film and a few minutes after it finished he heard his dad come up and go to bed. And then it occurred to him why Dad had brought that film home – it was Mum's birthday tomorrow.

Neither of them said anything about it as they went shopping and did all the other ordinary Saturday things, but they both knew what the other was thinking.

How old would Mum have been today? The question nagged at Danny all day. Thirty-eight? Thirty-nine?

How he missed her. Dad always bought Mum a big bottle of her favourite perfume on her birthdays. How great it would be to be able to smell the trace of that perfume in the house. How great it would be to be able to go up to Mum and hold her tight.

Yet, as the day went on, a feeling grew in him. Yes, he missed Mum, but he was sure that … what exactly? That she was at peace. Miss White was right. It was true what she'd said and Danny knew it now. Mum was at peace.

That night, he was woken up again by a noise. He sat up, wondering what it was. Another ghostly sound? He got out of bed and dashed to the light switch. The brightness calmed his nerves.

What was that noise?

He opened the door and listened. It was coming from his dad's room. There was no light under his door.

There, in the dark, Dad was crying.

CHAPTER SEVEN

Danny noticed Ryan as soon as he walked into the classroom on his first day at the new school. Ryan was sitting on his own, looking at a mobile phone.

Danny couldn't explain why, but he immediately felt there was something wrong about him. Ryan raised his head and Danny saw big eyes with dark rings round them. For an instant, Ryan's face seemed to melt away as if his eyes were staring out of a skull. A shiver ran down Danny's back but he blinked and the face was normal again. A sad face, but normal.

Two boys came over and started to chat to Danny. Harry and Brandon were friendly and spent the whole day helping him find his way around the school and introducing him to people. As they walked across the playground at the end of the afternoon, Danny asked them why they hadn't introduced him to Ryan.

'Oh, he's a weirdo,' Harry said. 'Doesn't talk to anyone. Only came here at the beginning of term. Stuck-up git.'

At the end of Danny's third day at school he got back to 13 Leylyne Road, dumped his school bag inside the front door and went round to see Miss White.

He sat in the kitchen while the old lady made a pot of tea and opened a packet of biscuits. Midnight brushed against Danny's legs and then jumped up on his lap.

Miss White beamed. 'See, he's getting used to you. Help yourself to biscuits, you must be starving. My mother always used to give me a jam sandwich as soon as I got back from school. So how have you been getting on the last couple of days?'

Danny started telling her about the teachers and the kids in his class and then the strange moment when he first saw Ryan. The old lady gave him a keen look and put down her cup of tea.

'You saw his skull?' she asked.

'I dunno – I thought I did. But it's stupid, isn't it? You can't see people's skulls.'

'No, most people can't,' Miss White said. 'But you can and you did. I knew it first time I saw you – I knew you had it.'

'Had what?'

'The Sight.'

Danny didn't want to hear this. It would just scare him. He jumped to his feet and told Miss White that he had to go because he'd forgotten something.

'All right, dear,' Miss White said. 'But you take care in that house. It's a bad place to have the Sight.'

He noticed that the hallway was chilly as he went inside number thirteen but he didn't pay much attention until he got to the top of the stairs and realised that it was very cold up there. His breath was steaming just like the other night when he'd seen those lights. Was it the same cold draught coming up from the cellar, like his dad had said? All the way up here?

He hurried along the corridor to his bedroom. It was warmer in there and he quickly closed the door to keep the heat in. He kicked off his shoes, changed into jeans and a T-shirt, then lay on the bed and switched on the TV. He would watch something and forget about Miss White and her mad ideas. Dad was right – she was a crazy old bat.

He was flicking through the channels when he heard a sound coming from the ceiling. Mice? It had happened once at their old house and Mum had been scared for weeks until Dad had set some traps up in the loft and got rid of them.

He listened again but the noises sounded heavier and slower than the quick little feet of mice. Then he jumped in shock at a loud thump directly above him. He reached for the remote and turned the TV down.

The noises had stopped. But there was a tension in the silence as if whatever had made the noise was listening too. As if it was holding its breath, waiting for him to make a move. Stupid! Stupid! There was nothing up there. He had to stop this. Had to stop getting himself scared about nothing. It was just his brain playing tricks.

He picked up the remote and turned the TV up. *Beach Days*. Great, his favourite soap, exactly what he needed: Australian sunshine and Judy Bradley, the best-looking girl in the universe, wearing a bikini.

He peered at the screen. Was it bad reception? There seemed to be another picture under the main one, as if a picture from another channel was coming through. What was it? A face?

He got up from the bed and went over to the TV. The picture wasn't any clearer. He peered closer and then shot backwards as huge eyes filled the screen for an instant and a voice exploded from the set. It was all so quick and the noise so loud and distorted that he couldn't be sure – but it was as if someone had called his name.

'Danny'.

Or was it 'Dandy'?

No, it couldn't have been that. It couldn't. That would be too scary.

He shivered, but it wasn't just fear. It was getting cold in here now too. The temperature was falling fast. He could see his breath, and the skin on his arms was rising in goose pimples. He grabbed a sweater and pulled it on. The air was so cold he could feel the flesh tightening on his face.

And now there was something else on the TV: a thick, gooey red was spreading down the screen. It looked like … like blood. Was it part of the programme? No, it couldn't be. It might be something they'd have in a horror film, but not on *Beach Days*. He grabbed the remote and changed channel. It was the same there. It was as if blood was running down the inside of the TV screen. He flicked back to *Beach Days*. The red streaks were almost to the bottom now, covering the whole screen and Judy Bradley seemed to be swimming through a sea of blood.

The hair at the back of his neck rose in terror and he switched the TV off. For a moment there was silence, then the thumping in the ceiling began again.

He dashed to the door and opened it. The air was freezing in the corridor. He took a couple of steps towards the staircase before the stench hit him. He'd smelled something like that before, when he had been walking along a footpath with some friends and they'd found the swollen corpse of a badger. Hundreds of flies had been crawling over it and the stink from the rotting flesh had almost made Danny and his friends throw up.

They had run away from the smell of death, and Danny ran now. Down the stairs, past the stained-glass window, to the door. He scrambled with the latch, trying not to breathe in the smell, then dashed outside into the night. It was raining hard but he kept going, down the path to the pavement. He couldn't stay in that house – he would ask Miss White to let him in.

He skidded round the hedge and screamed as he bumped into a tall dark shape.

CHAPTER EIGHT

'Danny!'

He stepped back and saw the figure was his dad, his umbrella raised against the torrential rain.

'What is it?' Dad asked, pulling him under the umbrella so that he could hear the rain drumming on it like the racing of his heart.

It all came out in a confused jumble – the cold, the noises, the TV, the stench. Dad stood and listened to him until he stopped.

'Come on, let's go inside,' he said, putting his arm round his shoulder and leading him towards the house. 'We'll sort it out together.'

Danny had left the door wide open and his dad tutted as he saw the puddle of rain that the wind had blown in on to the lino.

Dad sniffed and then sniffed again. 'I can't smell anything.'

He was right. The wind must have dispersed the stink.

'And it doesn't feel very cold to me.'

Again, he was right. And as they climbed the stairs towards his room Danny knew that there would be no strange blood on the TV screen and no strange noises in the ceiling.

Beach Days was finishing and there were the usual closing credits – no blood, no double image. And in the silence when he turned the TV off, there was just that – silence. No thumps.

'They were there,' he said, willing his dad to believe him.

'Tell you what,' Dad said. 'Let's go out and have a burger or something.'

They drove around in the pouring rain looking for a restaurant and finally chose a Tex-Mex one called Across the Border – mainly because there was a parking place right outside the door. His dad kept the conversation going throughout the meal but he didn't talk about what had happened until right at the end.

He took a big gulp of wine and asked, 'You OK now?'

Danny nodded and Dad smiled, reaching over and playfully pinching his nose like he used to do when he was young. 'I hate to think of you being all alone and scared in that house. But honest, Danny, you saw for yourself. There was nothing.'

'Yeah, but that place is haunted, Dad. It's not just me. Miss White said other people –'

'Oh don't bring that damn woman into it – she's a menace, filling you up with all this rubbish. Look, Danny, people only think they see ghosts and stuff like that when they're upset or emotionally disturbed. It's as if their brain gets confused and hysterical, so they take some small thing and turn it into something supernatural.'

'I'm not emotionally disturbed! And I'm not hysterical!'

'I know you're not. I know you're not,' Dad said quickly, glancing around the restaurant, and Danny realised that he had raised his voice – had, in fact, sounded hysterical. 'I don't mean that. But you've been through a lot, Danny. We both have. Losing Mum and Adam. Moving house, changing jobs and school. And it's come at the worst time for you – you know, growing up and everything. It's enough to make anyone imagine things.'

'I'm not imagining things and I'm not emotionally disturbed,' he said, trying to keep his voice calm and in control.

'Danny, I'm not saying you're crazy or something. All I'm saying is that you're … under pressure. You're stressed.'

'I'm not disturbed.'

'I know you're not. Danny, that's not what I meant. I know you're sensible, as sensible as they come.'

'So why don't you listen to me when I tell you there's a ghost in the house?'

'Danny – they don't exist. Ghosts don't exist. People die and that's it. That's the end. They've gone. They'll never come back. They'll never be seen again. Not as real people, not as ghosts, not as anything. And that's the … the terrible … painful truth. And all you can do is … somehow … carry on with life as best you can.'

There were tears in Dad's eyes. He poured the last bit of wine from the bottle and gulped it down, then stood up, threw some money on the table to pay the bill, and headed towards the exit. Danny followed him out into the driving rain. It was so heavy that he was soaked by the time he'd crossed the pavement and walked round the car to the passenger door.

Dad didn't start the car, just sat there, hands on the steering wheel, gazing at the rain streaking the windscreen.

'Listen, mate,' he finally said. 'If you prefer, we can go to a hotel or a B. & B. and get a couple of rooms.'

Danny shook his head. Dad had had too much to drink. Better to go straight home rather than drive around looking for a hotel.

'You sure?' his dad asked.

'Sure,' he replied.

Dad started the car and they drove through the deserted streets of the glistening, wet town. Back to that house. 13 Leylyne Road.

CHAPTER NINE

When Danny left school on Friday afternoon, Ryan was standing outside the gates, almost as if he had been waiting for him.

'Which way do you live?' Ryan asked.

Danny almost told him to mind his own business but it was the first time he'd seen Ryan speak to anyone at the school and he didn't want to be unfriendly so he pointed out the direction.

'I'm going that way too,' Ryan said and started walking with him.

Danny thought Ryan must have something he wanted to say to him but they walked in silence for almost five minutes. Danny tried to get a conversation going.

'What you doing this weekend?'

Ryan shrugged and they went on walking in silence.

A few minutes later, Danny tried again.

'Where were you before you came to this school?'

Ryan shrugged again.

The rest of the class were right – Ryan was weird. No wonder no one tried to be friends with him.

They were almost at Leylyne Road when Ryan finally spoke.

'I go this way,' he said, stopping suddenly and nodding towards the centre of town.

'OK,' Danny said, glad they were splitting up. But Ryan didn't move – just stood staring at him.

'What would you do if you were dying?' Ryan said.

'What?' Danny said in surprise.

But Ryan didn't reply – he gave Danny a long look and turned away. No goodbye. Nothing.

Danny watched him walk away and he almost couldn't believe what had happened. Had he really asked about dying? Or had he misheard it? Maybe he'd said 'flying'. Or 'lying'. What would you do if you were flying? But that didn't make any sense either.

Danny was still puzzling about it when he was sat in Miss White's kitchen later. The old lady asked, 'Have you started to make friends at school yet?'

Danny told her about Harry and Brandon. Then he mentioned Ryan and told her that no one liked him.

'Poor boy – he must be lonely,' she said, before adding, 'Talking of boys, have you got someone staying with you?'

'No, why?'

'Funny, I saw someone looking out of there today,' she said, pointing up to the side window.

'Who?' Danny said, as a shiver ran across his shoulders. He remembered the boy he had seen at the top of the stairs.

'I told you – a boy. Ten years old, maybe eleven, something like that. Same sort of colour hair as yours. Good-looking lad: angelic face, but a bit cheeky at the same time. You know, as if he was up to mischief. Friendly, though – he gave me a big grin and a thumbs-up then … ' Miss White stopped and leaned forward, 'Oh, lovey, whatever's the matter? You've gone all pale.'

The air seemed to have been sucked out of Danny's lungs and he had to take a huge gulp before he managed to say, 'That's Adam. My brother.'

Miss White's description had caught him exactly – his sweet face and his cheeky grin and that thumbs-up he always did.

When Adam was alive he'd really got on Danny's nerves at times and sometimes they'd had huge rows. But, deep down, they'd really loved each other. And Danny missed him now. Missed him terribly. He'd do anything to have him back: to hear him laugh, to be able to watch him playing basketball, to see the way he tugged the hair just above his ear whenever he was concentrating, even to suffer some of his teasing again.

'Do you think I could see him?' he asked, peering up at that empty window. The window of the room that Dad had called 'Adam's room'.

46

'Well you know, dear, I'm a medium, a clairvoyant, and I hear and see things other people can't.'

'I hear things in the house,' Danny said hopefully. 'And I saw some weird lights the other day.'

'Yes, I told you – a lot of people see and hear strange things in that house. Perhaps your brother will contact you, I can't say. But in the meantime I'll let you know what he says to me whenever he comes through.'

'Is he OK? I mean, is he at peace like you said Mum was?'

Midnight jumped off Danny's knees and scrambled up on to Miss White's lap.

'Who's getting restless? Jumping all over the place!' the old lady said to Midnight, stroking the cat's head and tickling his ears.

'Is he?' Danny insisted, feeling that Miss White had deliberately not answered his question. 'Is Adam happy?'

Miss White moved Midnight's head from side to side as if she was trying to decide the answer. The light from the window made her thin white hair glow like a halo. 'I can't be certain. I'd need longer contact with him. But my heart tells me he's not settled yet. I get the feeling he's still clinging to his old life here and he hasn't properly passed over to his new life on the Other Side.'

Danny went home after that and tried to ignore all the thoughts buzzing around inside his head. He listened to the radio as he fried some mince and onions and mashed some potatoes to make a shepherd's pie. Then he got out his books and started to do some Maths homework. When he had finished that, he opened his Science book but found he couldn't concentrate – he couldn't stop thinking about the face Miss White had seen at the window of Adam's room.

Was he there? Was it Adam who had been making all the strange things happen? Had he been trying to contact him? Was it his ghost that had been making the noises in that room? Was Adam's ghost there, waiting for him? The very thought made the hairs on Danny's arms stand up, but he had to go and see.

His heart was thumping hard as he started up the stairs. He glanced at the stained-glass window as he passed and, more than ever, he could sense the presence of the wolves, just out of sight, waiting to pounce on the sheep.

He reached the top and moved along the corridor towards the spare bedroom. Adam's room.

He stopped outside the closed door and stood very still, holding his breath, trying to hear any sounds from inside. He reached forward and started to turn the doorknob. At the last moment he changed his mind and let go. But the latch clicked and the door swung open on its own, as if inviting him to enter.

He took a few steps into the room and then stopped, shock fizzing through him and chilling him.

CHAPTER TEN

He had only glanced in here once, on the day they had moved into the house. Since then the whole room had changed.

On the wall above the bed were two posters – one of Batman and one of the Pistols basketball team – the same ones that had been in Adam's old bedroom. Two of his favourite books were on the bedside table, and his PlayMaster games were arranged next to them in a stack. His basketball shirt was hanging on the front of the wardrobe, just as it used to at home, proudly displaying the name ADAM above the number seven. His grey trousers, a white shirt and tie all lay neatly folded on a chair as if they were waiting for him to get up in the morning and rush off to another day at school. The little silver cup he had won in a fishing competition was on top of the chest of drawers and next to it was something that Danny had never seen before.

It was bigger than the cup and it looked like a brass vase but it couldn't be for flowers because the top was sealed. Danny picked it up and shook it. There was a scratchy, hissing sound from inside as if contained sugar or sand.

He had just put the vase back when there was a clatter from behind him and he spun round in shock. The pile of

PlayMaster games had fallen over. How had that happened? One of them was lying on the floor. He picked it up and smiled: it was *Dark Tower Quest*. Danny had never been very interested in video games but Adam had been a real expert and he'd loved *DTQ*, as he called it.

Danny looked at the drawings of the characters on the box. Adam always said the hero, Prince, looked like him. And it was true: older, of course, but with the same mop of hair, bright eyes and turned-up nose. And there, next to Prince, was his arch-enemy, Mefistoe, with his ugly face and cunning grin.

Adam had hated Mefistoe – almost as if he was real.

'He's the most evil bloke ever,' Adam always said. 'It's the hardest game in the world but one day I'm going to beat him.'

Danny was lost in these memories when he heard the front door open. Dad was home. He put the game back next to the others and dashed from the room. He didn't want Dad to find him there.

'Hello, mate,' Dad called out as Danny came downstairs.

In the kitchen Dad poured himself a large glass of white wine and began reading a newspaper while Danny checked the shepherd's pie in the oven and started heating the baked beans. He wanted to talk about Adam – about the way Dad had arranged the spare bedroom but he didn't dare. He tried to think of something else but everything reminded him of his brother. As he stirred the beans he remembered the silly rhyme Adam always sang:

Baked beans good for the heart

Baked beans make you fart

The more you fart

The better you feel

So eat beans for every meal

His dad interrupted his thoughts by holding up the back page of the newspaper and pointing to a photo of Adam's favourite basketball player, Shaun Hales.

'Says here he might be leaving the Pistols and going back to play in the USA. It would break Adam's heart if he knew. Do you remember how excited he was when he got Shaun's autograph? We waited nearly two hours for him to come out of the stadium but it was worth every minute. He was so nice to Adam – chatting and laughing for ages.'

They talked about other things during the meal but Dad obviously still had Adam on his mind and when he finished eating he smiled and leaned back in his chair. 'I wish I'd taken a photo of Adam when he turned round with Shaun's autograph. His face was lit up with joy – I can see it now.'

That did it. Danny couldn't hold back any longer.

'I went in the room,' he said. 'Adam's room.'

Dad looked down at the table and shrugged, 'I wondered when you would.'

'I didn't even know you had Adam's stuff.'

'I couldn't just throw it away, could I?'

'Yeah, but … why put it out like … like he's there?'

Dad shrugged again and shook his head gently as if he didn't know. 'Because I wish he was,' he said finally, then he pursed his lips together tightly and shook his head again. Danny was worried that Dad might break down and cry but he had to go on.

'What's that brass vase thing?'

Even as he asked it, he suddenly knew what Dad was going to say and he wished he hadn't asked.

'The urn? It's his ashes.'

Danny nodded and got up to leave the room. He needed to be alone for a while. He went to the front room and sat on the sofa.

So. Not sugar. Not sand. That scratchy, hissing sound he'd heard when he had shaken the vase was all that was left of his brother. All that life. All that flesh and blood and bone. All burnt and reduced down to … a scratchy, hissing sound inside a small brass urn.

He shuddered as he remembered how he'd held it up to his ear to listen to the sound. Adam.

When he went back into the kitchen his dad was still sitting at the table. He looked pale and he was staring away into the distance, at nothing.

'Have you got Mum's ashes too?'

'Yep,' Dad said softly. 'In my bedroom. In the little cupboard next to the bed. I say goodnight every night, and hello every morning. How crazy is that?'

'Why didn't you tell me?'

'I don't know. You never asked after the funeral.'

'I didn't know … I didn't think. Are you going to keep them?'

He shook his head. 'Grandad's coming down at the end of the month. We're going to scatter the ashes on the first of November. All Saints' Day. We thought it would be a good day to do it.'

'Where?'

'I thought we'd drive to Crossley Sands. We always had such good holidays there. Mum and Adam loved the sea … so it seemed like a good place to …' He trailed off and shook his head helplessly as if he couldn't bear to think about it.

'Dad, it's OK,' he said, hating to see him look so desolate and sad. 'Mum's at peace, I know she is. She's happy and at peace.'

Dad nodded bleakly, but Danny knew he didn't really believe it, almost wasn't listening.

'And Adam's still here,' he went on, desperate to make Dad feel better. 'He's with us, here in this house.'

'What?' Dad said, his face confused and shocked.

'Miss White's seen him. At the window upstairs. She saw him. She saw his ghost.'

53

'My God!' Dad shouted, getting up quickly and sending his chair flying. 'What the hell's the matter with that woman? I've lost my son. You've lost your brother. Isn't that bad enough? Oh no, now she says she's seen his ghost. God! What kind of torture is that? What kind of twisted mind has she got? We're doing our best to cope and she makes it worse. God damn her!'

'She's not making it worse. She's trying to make it better. She's going to talk to him and tell us what he says.'

'He's dead, Danny! He's dead.'

'But she's seen him. She told me. And she said what he looked like – and she got everything right: his hair, his face. Everything. She couldn't be making it up. She described him exactly.'

'Shut up, Daniel! Shut up!'

He flinched at the fury in Dad's voice.

'I'm sorry, Dan,' Dad said, reaching down and taking his hand. 'I'm sorry. I shouldn't have shouted. But I really don't want to talk about this. Let's just forget it, eh?'

They tried to pretend that nothing had happened but the memory of the row was like an invisible wall between them while they washed up and later when they sat together watching TV. Finally, earlier than usual, Danny said he was tired and went to bed.

As he was waiting to fall asleep, he heard a faint hiss in the darkness – like the sound of Adam's ashes in the urn or as if someone was whispering to him from the other side of the room. He tried to ignore it but it went on and on. Finally he pulled the pillow over his head to cut out the sound. And, at last, sleep came.

54

CHAPTER ELEVEN

When he went down for breakfast the next day he could see
Dad was in a bad mood. He hardly looked up – just grunted
quietly and went on reading the newspaper. Later, when
they were doing their weekly clean-up, he clomped around
the house with a grim expression on his face, dragging the
vacuum cleaner after him and carelessly knocking into the
furniture. Then Danny found out what it was all about.

'We're going next door,' Dad said as they were putting
the cleaning things away.

'What?'

'I want a word with Miss White.'

'I don't want to go.'

'I don't care what you want, Daniel. I'm going to sort
this out and you're coming with me.'

His stomach was churning with embarrassment as he
followed Dad next door; he knew what would happen – it
would end in another row. It would be awful.

To Danny's surprise, as soon as Miss White opened her
door and invited them in, Dad's dark mood seemed to pass.
He was charming and friendly. He said he liked her house,
admired the strange painting on the wall and even stroked

Midnight, though Danny knew he didn't like cats very much. He asked Miss White questions about her life and she chatted away happily. Even when she started talking about mediums and seeing ghosts he seemed really interested.

Suddenly he said, 'I hear you've seen my son.'

There was an innocent-looking smile on his face, but Danny heard the edge in his voice and realised that the friendliness had just been an act.

Miss White didn't hear it, though, and she began talking about the boy she'd seen in the window, describing him exactly as she had to Danny.

'Gosh, that's incredible,' Dad said. 'And you're sure it's Adam?'

'Oh, I'm sure all right. I knew who it was straight away,' the old lady said. 'And he's come through to me a couple of times since and we've had such lovely little chats. He's a sweet lad and you should be proud of him.'

'That's wonderful,' Dad said, pulling a photo from his pocket and passing it across to her. 'I thought you might like to see this.'

'Ah, look at him, bless him!' Miss White cooed. 'That's exactly the expression he had when I saw him the first time. Little Adam – such a sweetie.'

'Amazing,' Dad said, getting up and taking the photograph back from her. Danny saw the anger that burned in his eyes as he went on, 'Except that's not him. That's a photo of me when I was a kid. It doesn't look anything like Adam. You've never seen him – you're making it up. You're a liar and a fraud.'

He moved closer to Miss White, towering above her, so that she was looking up at him with confused, frightened eyes as he went on, 'And not just a liar. You're a cruel, wicked old lady. Danny is trying to deal with a terrible loss. Both of us are. And you're using that grief for your own twisted pleasure. Well, I'm warning you – it had better stop, right now.'

Dad walked to the door then turned, his face calm again and his voice gentle, 'Come on, Danny, let's go home.'

Danny wasn't convinced. When he got home he checked the photo. It was true that it didn't really look like Adam but there was still enough of a family resemblance to explain why the old lady had made the mistake. He didn't say anything, though, because he knew Dad had made up his mind. As far as Dad was concerned, Miss White was a liar and that was the end of it. Danny knew that he would never be able to talk about her or about ghosts again. He was on his own.

That night he was lying in bed, his head under the covers, when it sounded as if the door opened and clicked shut again. He lifted his head from under the covers but he couldn't see anything.

He lay back down, then –

'Na-night, Dandy.'

The words were there so strongly in his head that it was almost as if someone had whispered them in his ear. Not 'almost'. Someone had whispered them in his ear.

'Na-night, Dandy.'

Not someone. Adam. His voice.

'Dandy' was Adam's nickname for him. The name he'd heard when that voice exploded on the TV the other evening. He hadn't wanted to believe it then, but now he knew. And the eyes he'd seen on the screen, seen so briefly that he had hardly seen them at all, they had been Adam's eyes.

'Na-night, Dandy.'

When Adam was about five or six they had shared the same bedroom and every night Adam used to wait with the light on until Danny came upstairs to bed. Then Adam would switch off the light and whisper those words. A moment later he would be asleep, as if he felt safe now that his big brother was there to protect him.

The words went on running round Danny's brain. 'Na-night, Dandy.'

His mind was playing tricks, bringing back memories so vivid that they almost felt real. That's what Dad would say it was. But Dad would be wrong.

The thought terrified Danny, but he knew it was true: his brother's spirit – Adam's ghost – had just come into his bedroom. He had come in to be near him and now he was sleeping peacefully on the other side of the room.

CHAPTER TWELVE

'Your father's not a believer, dearie,' Miss White said when Danny went to see her after school on Monday. He had decided that he would still visit the old lady to talk about the spirit world, even though his dad disapproved. He would just have to be careful and never mention it to him.

'There are lots of doubters like him. It's not their fault – that's simply the way their minds work. They only believe in things they can see or touch, so they can't possibly accept that there's another world, another dimension. But we know better, don't we? Now, you say that Adam came into your bedroom – tell me exactly what happened.'

Danny told her.

'You see – I knew it. He's not at ease in his new world, he needs to come back to this world and see his big brother for comfort.'

Danny nodded, but he wasn't sure. It didn't fit. Yes, Adam had needed comfort when he was little, but by the time he died he was totally different. Grown-up. A pain, sometimes. Independent. And he definitely hadn't needed his older brother around.

Miss White bowed her head and there was a long silence before she spoke in a husky voice – 'He's here. Adam's coming through to me.'

A chill ran across Danny's skin.

There was another long pause before Miss White went on. 'I'm getting the word 'pay'. No, no – it's 'play'. Does that mean anything to you? 'Play'? Yes, that's what he's saying. Was he in a play at school or something? No? I don't know what he means. Perhaps he liked playing with you?'

Danny shook his head then had a thought, 'Maybe basketball – he loved playing basketball.'

'No, I don't think that's it.'

Miss White raised her head to the side, as if trying to catch some faint sound. 'What, dear? Swords?'

She turned to Danny, 'I'm hearing 'swords'. Was he interested in fencing?'

'No.'

'Oh no, he's fading away. He's going. I've lost touch. Oh dear, I wanted to hold on. Perhaps I was trying too hard.'

Danny felt as if he had been infected by his dad's doubt. He found himself watching Miss White closely, listening carefully to every word she spoke. All the things she was saying were so general and vague. 'Did he like playing?' 'Was he in a play?' She was just guessing. Fishing around. Of course Adam liked playing. All eleven-year-old boys did. And when she got things wrong – 'Oh he's fading away.' How convenient.

Danny felt he couldn't fully trust Miss White any more so he didn't drop in to see her the next evening after school. Instead, he went home, did his homework, prepared a meal and then watched TV. At one point he got up to check the meal in the oven but when he reached the door he heard an advert for a new video game. He spun round and stared at the screen. And suddenly it all fell into place. Why hadn't he thought of it before?

Of course Adam liked to play. Video games. He loved video games. He played them all the time. And now a tingle of excitement shivered across his skin as he thought about Adam's favourite game: *Dark Tower Quest*.

Swords. Of course Adam loved swords. He loved the sword fights against his enemy Mefistoe.

He had been suspicious about Miss White and it had stopped him hearing the truth. She had been right all along. She really had been in touch with his younger brother. And Adam really had been telling her about the game he loved to play.

All evening Danny worried away at it. What did it mean? Swords. Play. Was he telling Danny that he remembered playing his favourite game? Or that he still wanted to play? It was only when Danny was in bed that he saw another way of looking at it. Supposing 'Play' was an order? Supposing the message was for him: Play swords!

His whole body tingled because he had solved it. He didn't know why, but his brother wanted him to play *Dark Tower Quest*.

CHAPTER THIRTEEN

All day long he kept thinking about the game and when he got home from school he quickly prepared a meal and went up to Adam's room to get the PlayMaster and *Dark Tower Quest*. He took the console into his bedroom, plugged it into his TV, then sat on the floor and slipped the disc into the slot. His hands were shaking with excitement as he picked up the control pad.

Why did Adam want him to play this game? He wasn't sure what he was looking for – a message or something else?

The title came up. No extra words there. There was the short background story before the game. He almost skipped it but then he decided to watch it all the way through, in case the answer to the mystery was there.

The story was exactly the same as he remembered it – Prince's family are attacked in their castle by Mefistoe while Prince is out riding in the forest. When he gets home Prince finds his mother, brothers and sisters are dead. His father is dying but he has just enough strength to whisper the word, 'Revenge'.

Prince manages to escape and finds shelter in a monastery. One of the monks, Brother Dax, used to be a great warrior and he secretly teaches Prince the skills of fighting. Five years later, the seventeen-year-old Prince rides home. Mefistoe has taken over the castle and rules the country with cruelty and fear. Prince knows that the only way Mefistoe can be defeated is with Brother Dax's old sword, Regnum, which is hidden in the Dark Tower. Prince has to search for the tower, find Regnum and kill Mefistoe.

Was there a clue in the story? If there was, he couldn't see it. He'd only noticed two things. One, how ugly Mefistoe was with his horns and his weird face like a goat and his eyes that glowed with evil. He was much uglier and more scary than the picture on the box. And two, it was true – Prince really did look like Adam.

Anything else? Well, Prince's family had died. Was that it? Mum and Adam had been killed. Did Adam want him to take revenge? Surely not. And revenge on who? The train driver who had caused the crash by jumping a red light? He had died in the crash too. No, it couldn't be that.

It had to be something in the game.

He checked the game log. Adam's last game had been on 13 April. That number again. Thirteen.

13 April – the day before the crash. So Adam had probably played the game in the evening – a last game before the holiday in Wales. The last game ever.

And now a memory came rushing back. It was about the morning that Mum and Adam had left. They were waiting for the taxi to take them to the station and Adam had asked if he could go up to his room and play a game but Mum had said no.

'Oh go on – just five minutes,' Adam had said. 'It's important – I'm stuck.'

Mum had said there wasn't time and she was right because at that moment the taxi had arrived.

Mum had kissed Danny goodbye and walked away towards the taxi. Adam had said, 'Bye, Dandybum,' and followed her. So apart from those farewell words the last thing Danny had heard his brother say was, 'It's important – I'm stuck.'

Four hours later, he was dead. Crushed in the first coach of the train.

Tears filled Danny's eyes at the memory of that morning. The last time he'd seen Mum and Adam. He blinked the tears away and looked at the menu on the start page.

He selected PLAY GAME.

A picture of the tall dark tower came on to the screen, followed by a horrible cackling laugh, then the sound of a heavy metal door slamming shut. The words GAME OVER flashed up. The laugh came again before the screen went blank.

He pressed PLAY GAME again and again, but each time he got the same, words GAME OVER message. As he opened the top of the PlayMaster and took out the disc, he realised why Adam had said he was stuck.

He put the disc back in its box but he felt a bit as if he was letting Adam down. His brother's spirit had told him to 'Play swords' and he couldn't.

He had planned the meal for seven o'clock but Dad came back nearly an hour late. It was obvious he had been to the pub and had been drinking a lot. He was in a really bad mood and they hardly spoke while they ate. Afterwards Dad staggered to the front room, slumped down on the sofa, and fell asleep.

Danny went up to his room and did some Maths problems he had to hand in the next day. When he finished his homework he watched TV for a while, then he had another go at trying to play *Dark Tower Quest* – but it still wouldn't work.

As he turned off the console, he heard Dad come upstairs and go into Adam's room. A moment later there were heavy footsteps and his door burst open.

'Daniel!' Dad shouted.

'What?'

'What the hell have you done to Adam's room?'

'Nothing. I took a game, that's all,' Danny said.

'That's all? You've wrecked it – look.'

He followed Dad into Adam's room and was shocked by the mess. The books and games had been thrown all over the floor. The posters were hanging off the wall and Adam's basketball shirt was lying in a crumpled heap in a corner.

'I didn't do this. I just took the PlayMaster and a game.'

'Oh yeah? So this got done by itself, did it? It must've been you.'

He had been angry ever since Dad had come home late and now it all came bursting out of him, 'I did not do it! Get it through your head – I didn't do it, right? You probably did it yourself – you're so bloody drunk.'

'Don't you talk to me like that!' Dad shouted and raised his fist.

'Yeah – go on, hit me!' Danny yelled. 'That's what drunks do – punch people.'

Dad lowered his hand and looked shocked at what he'd nearly done.

'I'm sorry, Dan – I didn't mean it.'

'Oh yeah?' Danny said and walked back to his own room.

He slammed the door and locked it. A few minutes later Dad knocked and asked if he could come in but Danny didn't reply. He got undressed and went to bed. The row had been bad and he kept going over it in his mind until he finally started to drift off to sleep. Then another thought jolted him awake again.

He hadn't messed up Adam's room and he didn't believe Dad had either. In which case – who had done it?

There was only one answer – Adam.

CHAPTER FOURTEEN

Dad had already left for work when Danny got up the next day so at least the row couldn't start again. But the mess in Adam's bedroom, the PlayMaster and *DTQ* was on Danny's mind all morning. And then, during a European Studies lesson, he got a real shock.

The teacher was showing them a film about Paris and halfway through there was a shot of gargoyles on the cathedral of Notre-Dame. His skin tingled as, there, staring out at him was a statue that looked just like Mefistoe: the goat-like face, the horns and those cruel slitted eyes.

He dropped his pen in surprise. He bent down to pick it up and when he looked back at the film the scene had changed to the Eiffel Tower.

He was sitting in the hall at lunchtime, eating a sandwich, when Ryan sat down opposite him. The dark, dark rings round his eyes made Danny think of a skull again.

'Hi,' Ryan said. 'You looked like you saw a ghost this morning.'

'What?'

'During the film. That gargoyle – the one that looked like a devil. You went all white.'

'Get lost.'

Anyone else would have taken the hint, but not Ryan.

'Do you believe in them? Ghosts?' he went on, lowering his voice. 'What do you think happens when you die?'

'What? I don't know. Why ask me?'

Ryan looked at him for a moment, then got up and walked away.

'Weirdo!' Danny said, loud enough to be heard, but Ryan just kept walking.

At the end of school he didn't fancy going straight back home so he called in at Miss White's.

'Oh yes, dear, ghosts can do very destructive things,' she said when he told her about what had happened in Adam's bedroom. 'They can move things about in the house. Make things fly through the air. Break things.'

'Why?'

'Oh, usually to draw attention to themselves. But some of them – poltergeists – are just out and out wicked.'

That wasn't Adam. His young brother had always had a quick temper. Maybe he still had it now he was dead. But he wasn't wicked. Maybe he was angry about something and the only way he could show it was by wrecking his own room.

But angry about what?

The minute Danny asked the question, he knew the answer. Adam was angry because his big brother hadn't been able to play the game. But why was it so important?

Were there video games in heaven or wherever you went when you died?

'Do you know what happens after you die?' he asked Miss White.

'Nobody knows, my dear,' Miss White said. 'The veil between Life and Death is very thin but nobody knows what's on the other side of it. It's the great mystery.'

'Why? You talk to dead people. Don't they tell you?'

'Never. It's almost as if they're not allowed to. Or perhaps everything is so different in the next world that we wouldn't understand it. Perhaps there are no words to describe it.'

Danny could just imagine his dad's reaction if he heard her say that. He would laugh and think it was even more proof that she was lying.

It was all so confusing. His heart whispered that Miss White was right but he couldn't forget his dad's doubts. Perhaps this whole thing with *DTQ* was just stupid. Miss White had 'heard' Adam say 'Play' and 'Sword' and he had put two and two together and thought he had to play the game. But supposing he'd put two and two together and got six? And how much could he trust Miss White anyway?

'You know what I think?' the old lady said. 'I think some people have a peaceful journey across to the Other Side but that other people find it much harder. And Adam's one of them. Something's stopping him from crossing over.'

'Like what?'

'Perhaps he's scared. That's why he comes to your room every night.'

'I only said maybe he does. And, anyway, what would he be scared of?'

'Well, some people believe that our soul has to face a dangerous and difficult time after we die. That everything is so different on the Other Side that nothing makes sense at first and it's like being lost in the dark, surrounded by terrifying demons.'

'Do you believe that?' Danny asked, hating the idea that Adam was scared and lost.

'I don't know, my dear. I honestly don't know.'

CHAPTER FIFTEEN

As Danny was going upstairs after his visit to Miss White, something caught his eye at the side of the stained-glass window.

There was a dark patch, like a shadow, that he'd never noticed before. A trick of the light? He peered closer. No, it looked as if someone was standing just out of sight at the edge of the picture and that all you could see was his shadow.

It was hard to work out the shape but it looked as if the arms were reaching out towards something. Danny followed the line of the arms and saw something else he'd never seen before. There, just at the base of the mountains, was what looked like a small figure. It wasn't clear, but the more he stared at it, the more it seemed as if the figure was running. Running away? From what?

From the person standing just out of sight at the edge of the picture.

Chills began to travel down his arms. Now he'd seen it, the clearer it became in his mind. The small running figure was looking back over his shoulder, looking back in terror at the thing with the raised arms. Because when Danny peered closer and closer it wasn't the shadow of a person;

it was the shadow of a thing. A thing with hunched shoulders and folded wings and horns on its head.

The front door crashed open and Danny jumped in shock. He slipped and fell, banging the base of his spine as he slithered to the bottom.

Dad was in the doorway with a big grin on his face. 'What are you up to? Bit old for sliding down the stairs, aren't you?'

'You scared me.'

'Got off work early.' he said, pulling Danny to his feet. 'Wanted to get home to apologise about last night. I was out of order.'

'It's OK,' Danny said.

'No, it's not OK. You were right – I was drunk. And I said and did things I should never have done.'

'Honest, Dad – it's OK.'

'Whatever – I want to say sorry,' he said, ruffling Danny's hair. 'I still don't understand how Adam's room got in such a state, though. I wonder if a cat got in or something.'

Danny almost said it. Almost told him that Adam had wrecked his own room. But he knew that would cause another row. Dad didn't believe.

Then Danny thought of something that might make him believe.

'Dad, come and look at this.'

He led him up the stairs and pointed to the dark patch on the picture.

'What do you think it is?'

'A shadow?'

'A shadow of what?'

'A tree? Don't know.'

He didn't want to tell him what he thought it was but he traced the outline for him, pointing out the horn shapes, the folded wings and the hunched back, hoping that he would see it.

'Just a shadow. Could be anything.'

'And what about this?' he asked, pointing to the running figure.

'Looks like a flaw in the glass. Don't know. Could be a sheep, I suppose. What's all this about anyway?'

'It's not a sheep, Dad! Look properly. It's someone running away.'

'Really?' Dad peered closer and for the first time Danny noticed how deep the creases were round his eyes and how grey his hair had become at the side of his head. Dad stepped back and squinted at the window from a distance and sighed. 'Damned if I can see it.'

Danny was going to point out how the person was looking back over his shoulder but it suddenly didn't seem so obvious any more. He peered at the figure and was filled with doubt – perhaps it was only his imagination that made that light spot look like a face. He'd never be able to convince his dad if he wasn't even sure himself, so he let the subject drop.

That evening when he looked at the stained-glass window on his way up to bed he was even less sure – the frightening shadow, the running figure – his dad was right: it was all so vague, the shapes could be anything. He had been scared by nothing.

But when he turned the light off and got into bed his fear came flooding back. He had grown used to the feeling that Adam's spirit came into his room every night. It was comforting, and reminded him of the good times when they were young. Everything had been so much simpler, and much happier, back then.

He lay there waiting for Adam now. Waiting for that feeling that he wasn't alone. Waiting to hear his brother whisper 'Na-night Dandy'.

But when he felt something come into his room, it came with a breath of foul air and a chilling drop in temperature.

He opened his eyes and sat up.

Two bubbles of light, like the ones he'd seen that night in the hallway, were moving in the dark. They floated towards the wall, then up towards the ceiling. As they rose, they changed shape until they looked like distorted half-moons, like the slitted eyes of Mefistoe and the slitted eyes of the gargoyle on Notre-Dame. They stopped moving, stopped changing shape. Stayed there, staring down at him, examining him.

A slight breeze blew across Danny's face, like someone rushing past, creating a draught. The eyes turned as if they'd spotted the movement. There was a pause, then they zipped away across the room, leaving streaks behind in the darkness. They disappeared through the wall and the streaks faded away into nothing, like vapour trails dispersing in the sky.

He hated the thought but he couldn't stop himself thinking it – the draught he'd felt had been Adam. He had been hiding in this room. And when he'd run away, that other thing had followed. Chased him. Chased him like that shadow was chasing the small figure in the stained-glass window.

Somewhere in the darkness of the Other Side, Adam's spirit was running in terror, trying to get away from a monstrous demon.

The thought burned in his brain like a fever until his whole body began to heat up and he broke out in a sweat. He kicked off his duvet and let the cool air calm him down.

The lights were just headlights, he told himself. *The draught was just a draught*. He was being hysterical. Emotionally disturbed. Like his dad said.

He rolled over and closed his eyes.

It was chilly when he woke. He turned his head and saw that it was 1.55. He tried to pull the duvet over himself but his arm wouldn't move. It felt numb from the cold. He tried again and realised that something was clamped tightly round his wrist.

As he wriggled to free himself, he realised what it was – his wrist was being gripped by a hand. A cold, dead hand.

He screamed. Screamed and screamed while he struggled to free himself from that grasping hand. But it held fast, tightening its grip. And he screamed again and again.

The door opened and the light flashed on, blinding him.

'Danny – what is it?' his dad called.

He looked at his wrist and saw the red mark where he had pulled his hand free. He slipped it under the duvet.

'I had a nightmare,' he said.

'I should say you did. Frightened the life out of me!'

'Sorry. It's OK now.'

'Sure?'

'Yeah.'

He lay down again and let Dad pull the duvet over him.

'Sleep tight, mate,' he said, switching off the light and closing the door.

Danny had lied.

His dad would never believe the truth. Not about the cold hand gripping his wrist, and especially not about what had happened when the light had come on. The hand had let go and he had heard the whisper of a voice say, 'Dad.'

It had been Adam's voice.

CHAPTER SIXTEEN

'Has anyone ever played *Dark Tower Quest*?' Danny asked while they were waiting for their Art teacher to arrive.

He looked around the class and everyone was shaking their heads. Everyone except Ryan. He didn't say anything but he gave Danny a little nod. Just at that moment the teacher came in and the lesson began.

Why did it have to be the weirdo Ryan? He avoided looking at him at the end of the lesson but as he was getting his things together Ryan came over and said, 'Yeah, I've played *DTQ* a lot. Do you play?'

'I want to, but I can't. Every time I try, it says that the game is over.'

'Oh yeah – that means Mefistoe has won. You can only lose fifty fights, then he captures Prince and locks him in the Dark Tower.'

'You mean you can't play again?'

'No,' Ryan said, and Danny felt his heart sink. Adam must have lost fifty fights and now he was stuck. Stuck inside the Dark Tower.

No, not Adam. Prince.

Yes, but Adam had always thought of himself as Prince.

Maybe that explained everything. Maybe Adam was like one of those spirits that Miss White had talked about – the ones who were scared to cross over to the Other Side. But in Adam's case he wasn't just scared, he was also trapped. Trapped in the Dark Tower.

And that's why he wanted Danny to play swords. He wanted his big brother to rescue him. To set him free so that he could cross over properly and be at peace like Mum.

But how could he do that if the game was over?

'Are you sure you can never play again?' he asked Ryan.

'Think so. But I got to the end before I lost fifty fights. It's really cool when you get in the tower. There's a code thing you have to do before the sand runs out. It's all numbers and you have to add and take away before you can find the right one. But if you crack the code you can get this special sword to fight Mefistoe and win.'

Danny wasn't really listening. All he could think about was GAME OVER. Adam had said he was stuck. If Danny couldn't play the game for him, Adam would be stuck forever.

It all seemed hopeless. But the next morning, Ryan was waiting for him outside the school.

'I've found a way,' Ryan said, a big smile lighting up his usually sad face. 'I went on the Internet last night. There's this site where gamers go and discuss problems. I chatted to this guy in Sweden and he told me there's a cheat to get round the game-over thing. You have to create a new character. If you come to my place after school, I'll show you how to do it.'

Ryan lived in a flat over a shoe shop near the centre of town. They climbed the stairs at the back of the building but when Ryan put his key in the lock he stopped. 'You gotta promise something,' he said.

'What?'

'You won't tell anyone about me. About my secret. Promise?'

'OK,' Danny said, but he suddenly wasn't sure he wanted to go into the flat. What secret? Was Ryan even more of a weirdo than everyone thought?

'My mum's at work. She's never back till eight,' Ryan said, opening the door.

Danny almost turned round. Almost made up an excuse about why he had to go home – right now. But Ryan was the only one who could help him play *DTQ*, so he followed him inside and up some more stairs.

'My room,' Ryan said. 'You've promised, right?'

'Yeah, I promise.'

Ryan nodded and turned the handle. The door swung open and Danny saw the bed and a big poster of Judy Bradley on the wall.

'Hey – *Beach Days*,' Danny said. 'Do you like it?'

'Yeah, it's cool. I'd let Judy save me from sharks any day – as long as she's wearing that tiny bikini!'

Danny laughed. Ryan liked Judy Bradley. He'd even made a joke. Maybe he wasn't such a weirdo after all.

Then Danny saw the machine by the side of the bed. It had a screen and all kinds of switches and he thought it might be some sort of computer until he saw the bags of liquid and the tubes.

'It's a haemodialysis machine,' Ryan said before Danny could ask.

'A what?'

'It cleans my blood.'

'Why?'

'I got this virus three years ago when I was eleven. It messed up my kidneys. And now they don't, like, clean my blood properly – so the machine does it. This one's, like, really small and neat but the old one took up nearly half the room.'

'Do you have to use it every day?'

'Four nights a week while I'm asleep. It's OK really. Anyway, I won't have to do it much longer. I'm gonna get a transplant.'

'A new kidney?'

'Yeah. So I'll be, like, normal again. Or dead.'

'You won't die,' Danny said.

'People do. I've read all the stuff about it.'

Danny suddenly remembered those questions – 'What would you do if you were dying?' and 'What do you think happens when you die?' They'd seemed strange at the time but Ryan wasn't a weirdo at all. He was scared about what might happen to him.

'Why don't you want people to know?'

Ryan shrugged his shoulders, 'Just don't.'

Danny nodded. He understood. People asking

questions, treating you differently because you were ill. Talking behind your back about how you might die.

'I'll show you that cheat for *DTQ*,' Ryan said.

He put the disc in his PlayMaster and turned on his TV.

'Right. You skip the story bit and go straight to the menu – like this. But you don't press PLAY GAME. You go up to the top of the screen – here. See that shield? Click on it then press the X and A buttons at the same time and it brings down a little window. There you are. Then you type in the code. It's on that piece of paper on the side of my desk. Read it out.'

'XNAF3527TX009-1,' Danny said.

Ryan typed the code.

'Press X and A again and there you are.'

A new screen showed the Dark Tower. It looked ghostly, with a full moon shining down on it and a wild wind shaking the trees at its side.

'OK – here, the Swedish guy said you have to click on the flag at the top of the tower and you should get the option CREATE CHARACTER. Yes, there it is. Click on that, then choose a name. Write it in the box, click ENTER and you're in the first world. The Dark Tower is in the seventh world and you have to get there without losing all your lives. The only thing is, the guy told me you don't get fifty lives like in the main game.'

'How many?'

'Ten. Lose ten lives and you're out. And there are no more cheats. That really is game over.'

CHAPTER SEVENTEEN

Danny lost three lives on the very first evening of trying to play *DTQ*.

He did everything that Ryan had showed him and got to the page showing the Dark Tower – but it was different. When he went to click on the flag he saw a face in a window near the top of the tower. There were bars on the window and he realised it must be where Prince had been locked up.

He was sure the face hadn't been there in Ryan's game but then he realised why – it was only in Adam's game that Prince had been captured.

He looked closer at the face peering through the bars and Prince seemed even more like Adam than usual.

He had to get to the tower and free him.

He clicked on the flag and created the new character. It was a young man but he didn't look anything like Prince or Adam. Danny decided to call him Rusty, the name of a toy dog Adam had when he was little.

He typed in the name, then spent some time getting used to using the control pad to move Rusty around – making him jump and run and turn and crouch – before he set off along the path through the forest. He found a map at the base of a tree and it showed an arrow pointing to a cave behind a waterfall. He went there and found four weapons inside: a small sword, an axe, a mask of invisibility and a bow that fired flaming arrows.

He climbed the waterfall and came to a large lake. He spent ages trying to find a way across before he finally spotted a boat in the reeds. When he landed on the far shore he met the first of the enemies – five soldiers who attacked him. He put on the mask of invisibility and killed them all with the fire arrows.

He was so pleased with himself that he couldn't help punching the air and shouting, 'Go, Rusty!'

No wonder Adam had loved this game – it was fun.

Suddenly, night fell on the forest and wolves began to track Rusty. He shot flaming arrows along the path, setting fire to the trees and the wolves were scared and kept away as he raced along the track ahead of them. Then he ran out of arrows. He put the mask on but the wolves sniffed around and followed his trail. They surrounded him and closed in for the kill. Rusty disappeared under a pack or snarling, ripping wolves.

He had lost a life.

And he found himself back at the start of the game.

He played again, this time using his axe against the soldiers, so he had enough arrows to keep the wolves away until he got clear of the forest.

The sun came up and he was in a desert. Vultures circled, waiting for him to die of thirst, but he checked the map and found an oasis where he could drink and carry on.

83

He beat off attacks by snakes and hyenas and at last came to the edge of the desert and the end of the first world. He could see the wall up ahead. But the pack of wolves appeared again. They came racing down a hill trying to cut him off. He ran fast and got to the doorway in the wall just ahead of them. An old man came out of the door and raised his arms. The wolves stopped.

'You have two minutes to answer my riddle and pass through the gate into the second world,' the gatekeeper said. 'Two minutes and then I will set the wolves free. Do you understand?'

Rusty nodded.

'From the beginning of eternity to the end of time and space I am in every place there is. What am I?' the gatekeeper said, then he turned over a timer and the sands began to run.

Danny racked his brain trying to think of an answer. Beginning of eternity? End of time and space?

The pile of sand at the bottom of the timer was growing larger and the sand at the top seemed to be falling through more quickly. The wolves were starting to howl, getting ready to kill Rusty again.

End of time. End of space. In every place.

The sands were nearly running out.

And then he saw it. It was a trick. It was a letter. The beginning of eternity. End of time and space. In every place.

He typed the letter E in the answer box.

Yes! The door opened in the wall. The gatekeeper stepped aside. And Rusty walked into the second world.

Danny was thrilled, but Rusty had barely got through the door when a group of skeletons rose out of the ground and attacked him with swords. Danny panicked. He fumbled with the control pad and whirled Rusty around trying to fight off the skeletons but he didn't even have time to draw his sword. The skeletons closed in and stabbed and stabbed until Rusty fell to the ground.

He had lost a second life. And found himself right back at the beginning of the game.

He started off through the first world again but instead of wasting time looking for the boat to cross the lake he made Rusty dive in and start to swim. Everything went well until he was nearly at the far shore. Suddenly the water bubbled and boiled as hundreds of eels came to the surface and dragged Rusty down. They bit and tore at him until blood stained the water. When the eels swam away, Rusty sank to the bottom of the lake and lay still.

He had lost a third life.

Three lives gone and he was still stuck in the first world.

Danny turned the machine off. He was useless at video games, always had been and always would be. He would never be able to rescue Prince.

And anyway it was all mad. Adam wasn't trapped in the Dark Tower. Adam was dead. It was just this horrible house that made him have stupid ideas. The house and Miss White. His dad was right.

CHAPTER EIGHTEEN

The next day he didn't mention *DTQ* to Ryan. He didn't go and see Miss White when he got home after school. And he didn't allow himself to think about the house or Adam's ghost or any of the other stupid things that had been making him feel bad.

He cooked a meal. He chatted to Dad about nothing important. They washed up and watched TV together. Dad drank glass after glass of whisky but Danny didn't say anything to him. He didn't want a row. He just wanted everything to be normal.

He went to sleep and he had a good dream. It was Christmas. Mum and Adam were still alive and they were all living in the old house. Mum and Dad looked the same but Adam was only two years old and he was running about holding the cuddly dog he'd just been given as a present. Dad picked up Adam and swung him around. Adam laughed and Dad said, 'I've got a good name for your dog. We can call him Rusty.'

When Danny woke up, he opened his eyes and saw the *DTQ* box lying on the pillow next to him. He sat up and looked at it. It hadn't been there last night, he was sure of that. It had been on top of the PlayMaster.

Only one person could have put it there – Adam. It was a message. He wanted him to go on playing.

'I've lost three lives already,' he told Ryan when he saw him at school. 'And I'm still on World One.'

'Hey – bad news,' Ryan said.

'I got to World Two but when I lost it went back to World One again.'

'Didn't you save it when you got to Two?'

'I didn't know you could.'

'God, you're useless. Listen, I'll come and show you after school if you want.'

It was sunny when they got to 13 Leylyne Road and the house didn't look at all scary as they went inside. The sun was streaming though the stained-glass window and the colours lit up the stairs and even made the brown hallway seem bright and cheerful.

'Wow, cool place,' Ryan said. 'Awesome window.'

Danny looked at it and the picture wasn't at all creepy today. He couldn't even see the dark shadow in the dazzling light.

'OK – I'll show you how it's done,' Ryan said, picking up the PlayMaster control pad.

Danny thought about it. It didn't matter who rescued Prince, did it? Yes, it did. Adam wanted him to do it.

'No, I'll play – you just give me tips and stuff. OK?'

'Sure,' Ryan said and handed him the control pad.

It was much easier with Ryan giving him instructions. He told him quick ways of doing things, showed him shortcuts through the forest and where to find more arrows. In no time at all they were at the wall and the gatekeeper came out to ask the riddle.

'It's OK – I know the answer,' Danny said.

'No, they're different every time,' Ryan said. 'And sometimes they're really hard.'

Luckily, this one was easy.

'Peter's mother has three children,' the gatekeeper said. 'There's Nicholas and Penny. What's the name of the third child?'

It only took Danny a few seconds. 'Peter' he typed and the door opened.

'OK – quick,' Ryan said. 'Press X and Y and SAVE. Great – now you'll only go back to here if you lose a life. But you're not going to anyway.'

The second world was longer and much more complicated and dangerous than the first world but with Ryan's tips and advice he got through it safely. The only difficult part came with the riddle to get through to the third world.

'What is so fragile that you break it as soon as you say its name?' the gatekeeper asked.

Danny thought of glass things and china things before he realised it must be something to do with saying it out loud. The sands had almost run out when he got the answer.

'Silence.'

The door opened and he was in the third world. He saved the game and then decided he needed to stop. He felt exhausted from all the concentration, and his hands were trembling when he poured some Coke for them both down in the kitchen.

'It's hard work,' he laughed. 'But it's really fun with you helping.'

'You're not bad with the arrows,' Ryan said, 'but you're crap with the sword. You know there's a training room in the game? I'll show you. You can learn how to use all the weapons. And you can practise sword fighting with the fencing master. You ought to do it because the worlds get harder and harder, and when you have to fight Mefistoe in the Dark Tower he's, like, a real pro. I lost about twenty lives before I beat him.'

'OK. I'll practise all weekend.'

'You've got next week too – it's half-term, remember?' Ryan said.

'Oh yeah – can you come over and help me?'

'OK. Give me your phone number and I'll give you mine. The start of the week's all right but then my Dad's coming from Australia.'

'Does he live there?'

'Yeah. He and my mum split up when I was a baby and he met this Australian woman and went to live with her. He's never been back and I haven't even talked to him or anything.'

'Why's he coming?'

'He's going to give me one of his kidneys.'

CHAPTER NINETEEN

'I've hardly seen you all weekend,' his dad complained on Sunday evening. 'What the hell are you doing, up in your room all the time?'

His voice was slurred and there was a nearly-empty bottle of whisky next to his chair.

'Don't just shrug your shoulders – tell me what you've been doing.'

'Playing a video game.'

'I thought you hated them.'

Danny didn't know what to say. He could imagine Dad's reaction if he told him he was working on his sword skills for *DTQ* so he could rescue Adam. He shrugged again, hoping Dad would let it drop.

'Shrug, shrug! God, you're turning into a right moody teenager, you are,' Dad said, and Danny realised he was trying to pick a fight. OK – if he wanted a fight, he could have one.

'Have you drunk all that whisky tonight?' Danny said, pointing to the bottle.

'Mind your own business.'

'Why do you drink all the time?'

'Why do you waste your time playing stupid video games?'

'You didn't say they were stupid when Adam played them.'

'It was all right for him – he was just a kid.'

'Yeah, Adam was perfect.' As soon as Danny said it, he wished he hadn't. But it was too late.

'What's that supposed to mean?' Dad said.

'Nothing.'

'Come on, what do you mean Adam was perfect?'

'You never told him off. You always took his side if we had a row.'

'You sound as if you hated him.'

'Of course I didn't.'

'So why are you attacking him?'

'I'm not.'

'It sounds like it – saying I took his side.'

'You still do. He's dead. I'm alive. And all you can do is get pissed and think about him.'

'Don't be so bloody rude,' Dad shouted.

They glared at each other for a few moments, then Danny went upstairs.

He lay in bed waiting for Dad to come up but after a while he crept back down. Dad was asleep in his chair. His mouth was open and he was snoring. Danny left him there.

The next morning Danny woke up early but when he realised it was half-term he rolled over and went back to sleep. It was after nine o'clock when he got up and Dad had already left for work. When he opened the dustbin to throw away an empty milk carton there was a bottle of whisky inside. It was Dad's and there was still quite a bit of whisky in it. Had he put it there by mistake or was he chucking it away?

He thought about calling Ryan and asking him to come and help him play *DTQ* but he decided that he ought to do some more practice with the weapons first. He spent a couple of hours improving his sword skills, then he worked on spear throwing and hand-to-hand fighting. He was so caught up in it that he almost jumped out of his chair when there was a loud clatter from below.

He got up and opened his door. He held his breath and listened. Silence.

He tiptoed downstairs and into the kitchen.

Two saucepans were lying on the floor. A large carving knife was next to them. He put the pans back on the shelf and the knife on to the table. As he laid the knife down it began to turn, spinning fast. Round and round it spun until, suddenly, it stopped with the sharp blade pointing straight at him.

He ran out, slamming the kitchen door and raced upstairs to his room. He locked the door and sat on his bed, his heart pounding fast.

He tried to tell himself it was nothing. The knife had started spinning because of the way he had put it down. It was just chance that the blade had pointed at him. Perhaps. But how had the pans fallen off the shelf? And how had the knife stopped spinning so suddenly? It hadn't slowed down or anything. It was as if an invisible hand had suddenly grabbed the handle and stopped it so that the sharp point was aimed at his heart. Like a threat. A warning.

That was just ridiculous. Who would be threatening him? Adam's spirit? Of course not.

He tried to forget what had happened by going back to *DTQ* and practising his sword skills again, but this time he couldn't concentrate. All morning he had been winning his fights but now the fencing master kept rapping Rusty across the hand with his sword. When Danny clicked to exit the session, the fencing master did something that he'd never done before – he took off his mask. It was Mefistoe.

Danny shivered and turned the game off. His eyes ached from staring at the screen and when he looked at himself in the mirror they were bloodshot and his skin was pale and greasy. He needed a break from sitting in his room playing *DTQ*.

He went to the bathroom and splashed some water on his face. There was a sharp pain on the back of his right hand as the hot water ran over it. He looked down and was surprised to see three deep scratches. How had he got those? The carving knife? No – he would have felt it if he'd cut himself on the blade. He dried his hands carefully but the scratches stung and burned.

A thought flashed into his head – they had been made by Mefistoe's sword.

Stupid, stupid. That was impossible.

Yes, stupid and impossible. But he couldn't stop thinking it.

He couldn't stay here a moment longer, alone at 13 Leylyne Road. He ran downstairs and next door to see Miss White.

CHAPTER TWENTY

'Hello, dear. Haven't seen much of you lately. Come in,' said Miss White as she opened the door. She was holding Midnight and Danny went to stroke him but the cat hissed and jumped to the ground

'What's got into you?' Miss White said to the cat as Midnight scooted away down the hallway.

The cat was skulking behind the fridge when they went into the kitchen. Danny tried to tempt him out but he raised his paw and slashed at him.

'Ooh, naughty Midnight!' Miss White scolded. 'Leave him alone, dear. He's in a bad mood.'

They made tea and went into the living room. Danny was just raising his mug to his lips when Miss White pointed to the scratches on his hand. 'That wasn't Midnight, was it?'

Miss White peered closely at the marks while Danny explained how they'd suddenly appeared. The old lady tutted and shook her head.

'What?' he asked, alarmed by the expression on her face.

'I've been worrying about you in that house.'

Danny had a vision of the carving knife. The way it had

stopped with its blade pointing at him, as if wanting to stab him.

'Why?'

'Adam hasn't been coming through to me. It's as if something's stopping him. Something powerful.

Something … evil. Then the other day I glimpsed someone else at the window. It was gone in a flash but it looked like the Horned One.'

'Who?'

'The Horned One. The Devil has many names and many faces but this one has the face and horns of a goat.'

A shiver ran through Danny and he asked Miss White if she had a piece of paper and a pencil. He quickly did a sketch of Mefistoe. 'Does he look like this?'

'Yes, but uglier and more evil. Anyway, my dear, I want you to be on your guard in that house. And if you ever feel you're in danger, you just come to see me at once. If we stand together we are stronger than anything the Dark Side can send against us.'

The daylight was thickening into blue night when Danny left Miss White's house and went back to number thirteen. The two nearest street lights hadn't come on and the porch was dark as he fumbled around, trying to fit his key into the lock.

The air was chilly in the hallway when he got inside. He started up the stairs and stopped to look at the stained-glass window. The shadowy stain seemed to have grown larger and the top of the head definitely had horns.

It was as if the Horned One was creeping out from the Dark Side into the world. That was why the small figure next to the mountains was running away in terror.

He glanced back at the large shape and was frozen with horror. Instead of a dark shadow, it was now red. A red shape, and it was throbbing – throbbing like a beating heart that had been ripped out of someone's chest. And then the noise started. A deep rumbling that made the stairs shake. It grew louder and louder until he felt sick with the vibration that was filling his body.

His head began to spin and he turned to grab hold of the banister but his legs gave way before he could reach it and he felt himself tip sideways and fall.

The Horned One was there on top of him, pressing down on him, smothering him. He tried to fight back but his arms were weak. Fingers were clawing at him as if the Horned One wanted to rip his flesh away and drink his blood.

'Danny! Stop it! It's me. Calm down.'

The voice came through to him and Danny opened his eyes and realised that he had been fighting Dad. The front door was still open and he had obviously just come in and found him at the bottom of the stairs.

Danny sat up and grabbed Dad, holding on to him tight, still shaking from the shock. Tears were forming in his eyes.

'Danny, what is it? What happened?'

'I fell,' he said, then the tears brimmed over and slid down his cheeks.

Dad lifted him up and helped him walk into the front room. He sat on the sofa and Dad sat next to him.

'What is it, Dan? What's going on? Is it that old bag next door again?'

He kept asking questions, but Danny said nothing. He couldn't tell him what had happened – he wouldn't understand. He would say he was disturbed.

'Please, Danny. Tell me. Are you upset about last night?'

He shook his head.

'What then?'

'It's nothing. I just fell, that's all.'

'Look, Dan – I know I behaved badly last night. It was the booze talking – but that's no excuse. I feel terrible. You mustn't ever, ever think I loved Adam more than you. It's not true. You're my son – my first son. And I can't tell you how much I love you. If it wasn't for you, I couldn't carry on. You're everything to me. OK?'

Danny nodded.

'Good.' He smiled and ruffled Danny's hair. 'So are we going to eat tonight?'

'I don't know. I haven't cooked anything,' Danny said.

'Too busy playing video games, I bet!' Dad laughed. 'No probs – we'll send out for pizza.'

Dad poured himself some red wine when the pizzas came, but he put the cork back in the bottle and only drank one glass. Then they sat together and watched a film on TV.

Danny kept thinking about what Dad had said about loving him and it made him feel good, but he knew that it would still be impossible to explain to him about Adam and *DTQ* and the Horned One.

And he got proof of that at the end of the evening. He was passing the stained-glass window when he saw the dark shadow glowing red again.

'Dad, come and look!' he called. 'There's this weird light.'

Dad came running up the stairs and Danny pointed. But at that moment the red glow flicked off.

'It's the brake light on a car outside. Someone backing up and turning,' Dad said. 'Come on, Danny – you're jumping at shadows again.'

He was right – this time it was only a car's brake light. But last time it had been more than that, it had been something strange and mysterious. Like the threat of the carving knife. But he would never get Dad to believe him.

'Night, mate,' Dad said, giving him a kiss on his cheek. 'Sleep tight. Grandad'll be here in a couple of days – that'll take your mind off things.'

CHAPTER TWENTY-ONE

Ryan came round on Tuesday and he was really impressed with the progress Danny had made on *DTQ*.

'Wow – you're brilliant with the sword,' he said as Danny made his way through World Three, fighting off giant spiders and rats and Mefistoe's soldiers.

The riddle was quite easy too.

'In springtime I begin to put on my clothes,' the old gatekeeper said when Rusty got to the end of the world. 'In summer I am fully dressed. In autumn I start to strip. And in winter I am totally naked. Who am I?'

'It's the four seasons,' Danny said. 'Who's completely naked in winter?'

'Judy Bradley?' Ryan joked. 'I wish!'

'No, it's … Dressed in summer, naked in winter – it's a tree, I bet.'

He typed it in and the gatekeeper smiled and opened the door into the fourth world.

World Four was a world of snow and ice and mountains. Danny wasn't very good at controlling Rusty on the slippery slopes and a couple of times he nearly fell while he was being attacked by a flock of giant snow vultures that Mefistoe had sent. He finally beat them off with fire arrows but he would have been swept away by an avalanche if Ryan hadn't warned him to look up. He had just had time to duck into a cave before the snow crashed down. And even then he would probably have been killed by the bears who were hiding in the cave if Ryan hadn't told him they were there.

In fact, without Ryan he would never have made it through to the end of the world safely. And his friend was even more useful when it came to the riddle.

'Tell me the next set of numbers,' the gatekeeper said as he pointed to a row of numbers written on the wall.

1 – 11 – 21 – 1211 – 111221 – 312211 –?

'I know this one,' Ryan said. 'I had it when I was playing.'

'Don't tell me,' Danny said. 'I've got to solve it myself.'

But the more he looked, the less he could make sense of it. And the sand in the timer was slipping away.

'I can't do it,' he said. 'Dammit, I'm going to lose.'

'Can I give you a clue?'

'OK – a clue. But you mustn't tell me the answer.'

'After the first number, each new one tells you about the one in front of it.'

'What?' Danny said, starting to panic.

'Read out the first number.'

'One,' Danny said.

'The next?'

'Eleven.'

'Or?' Ryan said.

'One one.'

The sands were slipping away.

'Next?' Ryan said.

'Two one. Oh, I get it – there are two ones. So you put two in front of the one.'

'Yes!'

'And then there's one two and one one. And then there's one one, one two and two ones. Then there are three ones, two twos and one one.'

'Yes!' Ryan said. 'So what's the next line? Quick – the time's nearly up.'

'Er – there's one three, then one one, two twos and two ones.'

'Yes, write it down!'

The last grains of sand were slipping through the timer and the gatekeeper was about to let the wolves attack when Danny typed in the answer: 13112221.

The gatekeeper smiled and opened the door into the fifth world.

Danny pressed X and Y and Save.

'Phew – that was close. I need a break,' Danny said.

They went into the kitchen and made some sandwiches for lunch. It was a sunny day, and warm for the end of October, so they went out into the back garden to eat.

'You going to Harry's Halloween party on Friday?' Ryan asked when they finished eating.

'Yeah,' Danny said. 'You?'

'I can't – I'll be in hospital. Anyway, he didn't ask me. They all think I'm a freak.'

'Well, you're not,' Danny said. 'It's just cos you don't talk to them and stuff.'

'Yeah. Be different when I'm better.' Ryan stared at the wall at the end of the garden, then added, 'If I get better.'

'You will,' Danny said.

Ryan nodded but he didn't seem convinced so Danny decided to change the subject, 'Come on – let's do World Five. What's it like?'

'Oh, it's Sea World,' Ryan said, smiling again. 'It's my favourite – but it's hard. There're pirates, big storms … And you have to dive to collect pearls and there are sharks and a killer whale and these, like, mermaids with knives and nets and they try to drown you.'

Ryan was right – Sea World was hard – and very long. It took nearly an hour but Danny got through all the dangers and tests and, at last, he arrived at the wall. The gatekeeper stepped forward and set the riddle:

'Forward I am heavy, but backwards I'm not.'

Danny saw it at once – 'Backwards it's NOT, so forward it's TON.'

He typed it in and Rusty walked through into World Six.

Danny saved the game and turned off the PlayMaster.

'Oh well, I ought to go,' Ryan said. 'We're picking my dad up at the airport this evening. How weird is that? Never met him but in a couple of days he's going to give me a kidney.'

'Can't anyone else give you one?'

'They can but it's best if it comes from someone in your family. Mum was going to do it but she's got this rare blood group. So she wrote to Dad and he said yes. I guess he must love me or something.'

'Course he loves you. He's your dad.'

Ryan thought about this for a moment, then he smiled. 'Yeah … So you're going to have to finish *DTQ* on your own.'

'Oh I don't know – maybe I'll wait until you get out of hospital. I've got my Grandad coming soon anyway.'

Danny walked into town with Ryan. He didn't know what to do when they said goodbye. Shake hands? Hug him? In the end he just punched him lightly on the shoulder and said, 'See ya!'

'Yeah,' Ryan said, returning the punch.

'I'll come and see you in hospital.'

'Yeah, OK,' Ryan said, then he climbed the steps up towards his flat.

CHAPTER TWENTY-TWO

Danny went to the station with Dad to meet Grandad. It was the first time Danny had seen him since Mum and Adam's funeral and he'd grown thinner and older. But his hug was warm and Danny was really glad he was there.

They had got back to Leylyne Road and were walking up the path to the house when Miss White called out from her front porch. 'Danny, have you seen Midnight? He's been out all day and he's still not back.'

'No, sorry. I'll let you know if I see him.'

'Who's Midnight?' Grandad whispered as they went in through the front door.

'Our neighbour's cat,' Dad said. 'Miss White and her black cat. The old witch has been filling Dan up with all sorts of superstitious nonsense. She needs locking up.'

Grandad took his coat off and shivered as he hung it up on the peg.

'This is a chilly old house, Stuart. Gloomy too. When are you going to get your own place?'

'As soon as we find one,' his dad said.

'The sooner the better, if you ask me. This place feels odd.'

'Oh not you, too, Mark! You're as bad as Daniel. It's just an ordinary house. Bricks and mortar, for goodness' sake.'

But Danny was delighted that Grandad agreed with him and he was looking forward for a chance to talk to him about things – he would understand.

It was comforting to go to bed that night knowing that Grandad was next door, although Danny wondered what he'd thought when he'd seen that the room had been turned into a kind of shrine to Adam.

'I had a really vivid dream last night,' Grandad said when he and Danny were eating breakfast the next morning. 'About poor little Adam. Dreamed he was there, talking to me. Felt so real, I woke up with a terrible ache in my heart.'

It was just the opportunity Danny had wanted and he started telling him about Adam's spirit coming to his room, and about the evil presence and the things Miss White had told him about the house. He even told him about the stained-glass window and took him up to look at it. He was disappointed when Grandad couldn't really see the shapes but at least he didn't say it was nonsense the way Dad had.

'No, of course, it's not nonsense,' he said. 'But that Miss White woman sounds like a superstitious nutter.'

'And I suppose Dad isn't superstitious?' Danny said. 'The way he's put all of Adam's things in the room as if he's still alive? And he's drinking like mad.'

'Is he? He only had one glass of wine with our meal last night.'

'Yeah, but you should see him when he's drunk.'

'Look, Danny, we all have our own ways of trying to deal with our grief. Your gran has been dead five years but her clothes are still in the cupboard where she left them. Just can't bring myself to get rid of them. And since your mum died, I've dug out all the old photos of her and the drawings she did when she was a little kid and I spend hours looking at them. It's the hardest thing on earth, to lose the ones you love. My wife, my daughter and grandson …' His face creased with pain and tears filled his eyes as he added, 'If only your Mum and Adam hadn't been coming to visit me, they'd be alive today.'

'Grandad, don't say that! It's not your fault the train crashed. And they wanted to see you. You know how much Mum loved you. And Adam was so excited – he'd talked about it for weeks before.'

His grandfather took out a hanky and blew his nose and wiped his eyes, but the tears continued to run down his lined face. It was awful seeing him upset like this so Danny suggested going out for a walk around town.

He showed him all the sights and they visited the Pines Shopping Centre. He was dying to talk some more about all the weird things that had happened at 13 Leylyne Road but he didn't want to mention anything that might upset him.

But in the end Grandad was the one who brought it up.

'I really don't like that house,' he said as they were having a drink in a cafe. 'Whatever your dad says, it's definitely got an odd feel.'

'Do you believe in ghosts, Grandad?'

'Ghosts? I don't know. Sometimes I get the feeling that your gran is right there beside me. But that's not really supernatural, not like some transparent ghostie going around with its head under its arm!'

'What about last night – Adam talking to you?'

'That was only a dream. Hey, no need to look so disappointed.' He chuckled and ran his finger down Danny's cheek. 'You looked just like your mum for a moment. I'm so lucky – she lives on in you.'

Danny was reminded of what Miss White had said about his mum being a part of him. Maybe it was true.

'As for ghosts,' Grandad went on, 'who knows what happens to us when we die? One thing's for sure – the world's a much stranger place than it seems. I read an amazing book about the universe the other day. It explained that all the things we see and feel are made of matter that "shines", meaning it can be detected as heat or light or X-rays or radio waves. Well, apparently, they now know that there's matter that can't be detected like this. They know it's there because it has gravity, but it doesn't "shine", so they call it "dark matter". And there's four times as much dark matter in the universe as there is of the matter we can see.'

Danny remembered Miss White talking about the Dark Side and he wondered if that had anything to do with dark matter.

'Not only that,' Grandad continued, his face alive with excitement, 'but now they've found something they call "dark energy". It's not matter, and it's not gravity because gravity pulls and this dark energy does the opposite – it pushes! I mean I can't understand half of this stuff but if there's all this dark matter and dark energy that we can't see or feel or hear, who knows what else is going on. Maybe there's another universe right next to us and we can't see it. Maybe that's where we go when we die. And maybe sometimes things cross over from that universe and we call them ghosts.'

Grandad raised his cup to his lips and drained the last of his coffee, then gave Danny a big smile. 'It's a funny old world.'

CHAPTER TWENTY-THREE

Danny got a text from Ryan early on Friday morning:

Hospital sucks. But my dad is SO cool. It's the big day 2day. X your fingers for me + him. Have gr8 halloween party 2nite.

Danny remembered the way Ryan's face had looked like a skull the first time he'd seen him. Miss White had said it meant he had the Sight. If she was right maybe it meant that Ryan was going to die.

He crossed his fingers and closed his eyes, wishing with all his might that the operation would work and everything would be OK.

Dad had taken the day off and after lunch he and Grandad got ready to drive down to Crossley Sands.

'I wish you were coming with us,' Grandad said. 'Your dad's booked the caravan where we all used to stay.'

'I know. But I've got this party tonight. Dad said I could go weeks ago.'

'And you're sure Harry's parents said you could stay the night?' Dad said, putting a bag in the boot of the car.

'Yeah. We're all going to kip on the floor. It'll be a laugh. Then I'll catch the train first thing.'

'So you'll be there when we scatter the ashes? Grandad said.

'Of course,' Danny said, looking at the two urns lying side by side on the back seat of the car.

Grandad sighed with relief and gave Danny a hug. 'It wouldn't be the same without you.'

'OK then – we'll get going,' Dad said. 'Now, no drugs – promise.'

'Come on, Dad – I'm not stupid.'

'And no booze.'

'You can talk.'

Dad laughed and pretended to clip him round the ear. 'That's over. I mean it. OK?'

Danny smiled and nodded.

He watched as they drove away and then he went back into the house. He stood by the front door and listened – it was very still and quiet. Almost too still and quiet. As if the house was waiting – waiting for something to happen.

He went up to his room and turned on the TV so there would be a bit of noise. He watched an episode of a stupid soap and a game show, then he switched over to a film. It was OK for a while but the story started to get a bit creepy so he switched it off and put his headphones on to listen to music while he surfed the Internet. About ten minutes later he took them off again – in case he couldn't hear if there was a strange noise in the house.

That was a stupid thing to think, because now, when he listened, he could hear strange noises everywhere. He was spooking himself. Stop it! They were just ordinary noises.

He checked to see if any of his friends were online. No one. He thought about doing some more sword practice for *DTQ* but the truth was he didn't want to go on being alone in the house.

He ran downstairs and went next door to see Miss White.

She had deep, dark rings under her eyes and she was very pale so he asked her if she was all right.

'I haven't been able to sleep,' she said. 'Midnight's not coming back. I can feel it in my bones.'

'Don't worry, cats often go off for days,' he said.

Miss White shook her head, 'Not Midnight. Something's happened to him, I know it has.'

She sat in her chair, staring out of the window as darkness fell. Danny was used to her silences and, since he would rather be with her than alone in number thirteen, he stayed and made them both a cup of tea.

While they sipped the tea he tried to cheer her up by talking about anything that came into his mind – school, Grandad, even how he'd been playing *DTQ*. He could see she wasn't really listening but when he said was going to a Halloween party she turned to look at him.

'It's not Halloween,' she said. 'It's proper name is Samhain. And it's not a time for having parties. It's dangerous!'

'Why?'

'Because it's the end of the lighter half of the year and the start of the darker half.'

'Why's it dangerous?'

'It's the night when the border between this world and the Other Side becomes thin. Thin enough for spirits to pass through. Harmful spirits and harmless spirits. They can come. And they can go. People understood that for thousands of years, but now it's just an excuse for stupid things like trick or treat and dressing up as witches. Halloween – rubbish.'

She turned back to stare through the window at the dark black night outside and Danny decided he didn't want to stay with her any longer. It was nearly time to get ready for the party anyway so he went back to number thirteen.

He dressed quickly, cleaned his teeth, splashed on some of his dad's aftershave, and was out of the front door in just over five minutes. He was early but it would be better to be out on the street than alone in that house.

CHAPTER TWENTY-FOUR

He walked slowly though town but it was still only seven o'clock when he got to Harry's house. He waited further down the road for nearly a quarter of an hour until he saw a group of people go inside. He hurried over and rang the bell.

Harry opened the door. He was dressed as a vampire and Danny could see that everyone else was dressed up too.

'I didn't know it was fancy dress,' he said.

'Doesn't matter – you look scary without dressing up!' Harry laughed, dragging him inside. 'Hey, guess what? My parents have had to go and stay with my gran. They left my brother Connor in charge and he's only gone and asked all his mad college mates round. It's gonna be a riot!'

Danny was the only one not in a Halloween costume and he felt out of place in the middle of all the witches and monsters so he drank a can of beer hoping it would make him feel less embarrassed. But it didn't. He thought about having another but he remembered his promise to his dad – and, anyway, he didn't like the taste very much.

More and more people arrived and they crammed into the front room and the hallway, drinking and dancing to the loud music. Danny wanted to join in but he couldn't. It would be OK if he was dressed up as Dracula or something but he would only feel stupid dressed like this. He sat on the stairs and watched everyone dancing and running around trying to scare each other.

Some of the costumes were really frightening. One of the older boys had a plastic eye with a nail sticking out of it and some kind of fake blood kept trickling down his cheek. There were people who wore the mask of the murderer from the movie *Scream* and others were dressed as Frankenstein monsters, devils, witches, skeletons, aliens and zombies.

For a long time dance tracks blasted out of the speakers but now it changed to trance music and someone turned on a strobe light. The flashes made everyone's movements seem strange and jerky and the music was like something from another world. From the middle of the crowd came a tall figure. It was moving slowly and waving its arms. The lights flashed off and on so fast that Danny couldn't believe what he was seeing.

The horns. The goat face. The eyes like huge dark slits.

It was Mefistoe.

It was the gargoyle.

Danny stood up, getting ready to run as the creature came closer, heading straight towards him. It came from the front room and pointed a long claw at him.

But a moment later it lifted up the mask and there was Brandon grinning up at him.

'You should have seen your face – you looked like you were going to mess your pants!' Brandon laughed, then lowered the mask and staggered back into the crowd of dancers.

It was only Brandon. Only a joke. But it had still been a shock and for a moment it had seemed as if it was real. As if Mefistoe had come across from the Other Side. Because Miss White said that's what happened at Samhain – spirits could cross from one world to another.

She had also said that Halloween was rubbish. And that it was a dangerous time because the border between the two worlds was thin. He hadn't really paid much attention at the time but now it seemed very important. Like a message.

Tonight, the border was thin. Tonight, spirits could move from this world to the Other Side. Well, if that was true – tonight would be the best time to help Adam escape from the Dark Tower. Tonight, his young brother might be able to make his journey over to the Other Side – to where Mum was waiting for him.

It scared him to think about going back to 13 Leylyne Road, especially tonight. Because Miss White had said that the thin border allowed harmful spirits to come into this world too.

It scared him.

But he had to go.

CHAPTER TWENTY-FIVE

There was no moon and no stars and 13 Leylyne Road was totally dark as he stood looking at it from the road. Dark and scary. He really didn't want to go in there.

He went next door to Miss White's instead. He would tell her what he was going to do. She knew about the Dark Side – perhaps she could give him some advice or help.

But Miss White was in no state to help anyone. When she opened the door she looked as if she had aged years. Her cheeks were sagging and her eyelids were red as if she had been crying. Her hands were trembling and she shuffled slowly, reaching out to steady herself against the wall as they made their way to the kitchen. Once there, she slumped down on a chair.

'What's the matter?' Danny asked.

Miss White half raised her hand and pointed to the table. Newspapers were spread across it and there was a large blue towel in the middle. There was a lump under the towel and Danny guessed what it was even before he lifted it.

He was expecting to see Midnight's body, but he wasn't prepared for the four long claw marks that had ripped through the fur of the cat's belly, opening him up from his throat to his rear legs. Danny stepped back and let the side of the towel drop and cover the mangled body and the bloodstained newspapers.

'I told you!' Miss White said. 'I knew he was dead.'

'Where was he? Who did it?' Danny asked.

'On the roof of my shed, poor little thing. Mr Landis next door reckons he was attacked by a badger. A badger! How would a badger throw him on top of the shed? I know the work of evil when I see it.' Miss White turned and pointed her finger at Danny's house. 'I told you I saw that cruel face in the window. That's who killed Midnight. That house is evil and it draws evil to it. Your father ought to be ashamed of himself, leaving you alone there! Tonight of all nights.'

Danny didn't want to listen to her criticising his dad, so he headed for the door without saying goodbye. Forget Miss White and her rudeness. She was just a sad old lady who had lost her cat. Mr Landis was right – an animal had killed Midnight.

But as Danny turned his key in the lock of 13 Leylyne Road he couldn't forget those warning words. That house is evil.

The door swung open and he went inside. He switched the light on in every room, even the cellar – he didn't want any part of the house to be dark. When he was sure that there was nobody hiding anywhere he went to the front door and locked it, then checked that the back door was bolted too. He opened the small cupboard in the kitchen and took the big hammer out of his dad's toolbox. Just in case.

He tried not to look at the stained-glass window as he climbed the stairs, but out of the corner of his eye he saw that the shadow had grown larger and seemed to loom over the small figure cowering near the mountains.

At the top of the stairs the air was cold and it got even colder as he walked to his room. But he couldn't turn back now. He had to go on. He had to play the game. He had to free Prince. Because that would free Adam. Nothing must be allowed to frighten him. He had to concentrate and play better than he had ever played.

In his room he put the hammer down next to his chair, plugged the console into the TV, and slipped the disc into place. The machine whirred and, while the information loaded and the titles started to run, he went to Adam's room. He took the basketball shirt off the hanger and slipped it over his head. It might inspire him to play better. The shirt was small for him and he could just imagine what Adam would have said if he'd seen him: 'Hey, get your smelly armpits out of my shirt or I'll puke up!'

Back in his own room he took out a couple of thick sweaters and pulled them on to protect him from the freezing air, then he sat down in front of the screen. He picked up the control pad and pressed Play Game.

He still had seven lives left. Seven lives to get through World Six, find the sword, Regnum, and kill Mefistoe.

'OK, Rusty,' he said out loud, 'let's do this.'

CHAPTER TWENTY-SIX

He lost two lives in the first ten minutes.

It felt so different without Ryan there to give him advice and his fingers were tense and clumsy on the control pad.

'Come on, take it easy. Relax,' he said out loud as he started World Six again.

There was a long, long rope across a canyon and, for the third time, he started to move Rusty along it. A wind was howling and the rope was swinging backwards and forwards so it was difficult to keep Rusty balanced. But, bit by bit, he edged him closer and closer to the other side. He was almost there when an eagle attacked. It dived down and knocked Rusty off the rope and he fell to the rocks below.

Only four lives left now and he was back at the start of World Six again.

This time he remembered the advice Ryan had given him – always look around to see if there's anything to help you. He walked Rusty along the clifftop and came across a long stick lying on the ground. That's what tightrope walkers always used. He picked it up and went back to the rope and started across. It was so much easier to keep his balance with the stick and when the eagle dived he used if to scare the bird away. Four more steps and he was standing safely on the far cliff.

He pressed P<small>AUSE</small>.

His hands were sweaty and he wiped them on his jeans. He had to stay calm and take his time, the way Ryan had taught him.

He thought of his friend, lying in the hospital. Was the operation over? Had it worked?

He breathed deeply and set off across the mountains, through World Six. It was a difficult journey and he had to fight off attacks by wild animals and Mefistoe's soldiers but at last he came to the wall. The old gatekeeper came out and set the riddle:

'I have been here for millions of years but I am never more than a month old. What am I?'

The sands began to run through the timer. What's been here for millions of years? The sea? Rocks? Air? Yes – but never more than a month old …? Something that was born every month? Or changed every month?

The sands were almost gone when he got it. The moon.

He typed it in and the door swung open.

He stepped through and there in front of him was the Dark Tower.

Only one small light showed in that tall building, which seemed to reach up to the sky. There, right near the top, a light shone from a small window with bars across it. And inside, waiting to be rescued, was Prince.

Danny pressed X and Y and S<small>AVE</small>.

He was here, at last, ready to face Mefistoe. Ready to fight him and set Adam free.

At that moment he heard someone coming up the stairs.

CHAPTER TWENTY-SEVEN

Danny held his breath and listened.

The footsteps reached the top of the stairs. A floorboard creaked. He heard the door to Adam's room open and close. He picked up the hammer and went out into the corridor. Suddenly the light went out. He looked down the staircase – it seemed that every light in the house was off. He gripped the hammer tight and tiptoed along to Adam's room and opened the door.

Light was shining in from the street lights and the room seemed empty. He checked under the bed and in the cupboard. No one.

He went back to his room and locked the door. He tried the light switch but nothing happened. And yet the TV was still working. Perhaps the fuse for the lights had blown. He didn't fancy going down to the cellar to check. Better to stay here and at least he could keep playing the game.

He picked up the control pad and began moving Rusty along the path towards the Dark Tower and then through the archway into the courtyard. There in a huge iron cage stood a long shiny sword – Regnum. Across the lock of the cage was a series of numbers, 1 – 16 – 8 – 23 – 15 – 30 – ? –

?, and underneath was a message: FIND THE MISSING NUMBERS TO SOLVE THE CODE AND OPEN THE CAGE.

As he looked at the numbers a small timer in the cage tipped upside down and the sands began to slide into the bottom half. How long did he have?

He stared at the numbers. He couldn't see what he had to do.

The sands were slipping through.

And then he remembered that Ryan had said something about these numbers when he had first talked about *DTQ*. What was it? Something about adding and taking away.

He jumped in shock as a loud bang shook the door of his bedroom.

He picked up the hammer and went to the door.

It sounded quiet outside so he unlocked it and slowly turned the handle. The door swung open.

It was dark but he could see there was no one there. And yet … when he listened … was that the sound of soft breathing? Close, as if someone was standing right in front of him, there was a puff of hot air on his face.

He slammed the door and locked it again.

When he got back to the TV screen he was just in time to see the last few grains of sand fall through the timer. A loud laugh rang out from the Dark Tower. He had lost another life.

The bedroom light flashed back on.

It had all been a trick to make him lose. Now he only had three lives left.

He started back outside the Tower and made his way into the courtyard again. There was Regnum in the cage. But the code had changed and it looked much harder: 17 – 83 – 73 – 139 – 129 – 195 – 185 – ? – ?

The sands began to fall through the timer.

Ryan had said you had to add and take away. OK – it went up from 17 to 83, then down to 73, then up to 139. So there was adding and taking away.

The light flickered and a tapping started in the wall. Tap. Tap. Tap. Not loud but fast. On and on.

It was another trick to make him lose.

What was the gap between 17 and 83?

Tap, tap, tap, tap.

Don't listen. Think. Concentrate. The gap between 17 and 83 … was 66. OK. Then from 83 it went down to 73 – so that was minus 10. Add 66 to 73. That came to – 139.

Tap, tap, tap, tap. The tapping was getting louder.

Concentrate.

The sands were racing through the timer.

OK, minus 10 from 139. That was 129.

Good. So it was always add 66, then subtract 10.

Tap, tap, tap, tap, tap, tap.

The light was flicking on and off.

It was impossible to think.

So he needed to add 66 to 185.

The sands were running out.

185 plus 66?

251.

Minus 10?

241.

He typed in the numbers 251 and 241.

The door of the cage swung open and Rusty reached in to grab Regnum.

The tapping stopped. The light stopped flickering.

There was a roar from inside the Dark Tower. The roar grew louder. Someone was coming.

He turned Rusty round and stood there, with his sword at the ready.

CHAPTER TWENTY-EIGHT

The roaring and growling grew louder and Mefistoe burst out of a doorway into the courtyard.

He was far uglier than the picture on the box and much more like the grinning evil face of the gargoyle. He was carrying a sword and blood was dripping off the end of the blade.

Danny immediately thought of the long wounds in Midnight's belly. Maybe he hadn't been ripped by claws. Maybe the marks had been made by cuts from a sword.

Mefistoe charged. Danny waited and then, at the last moment, he made Rusty step aside and slash with his sword. It was something he had learned to do in training and it had always worked against the soldiers but Mefistoe didn't fall for the trick – he simply ducked and Rusty's sword swished through empty air. The next moment Mefistoe stepped forward and stabbed him in the chest. Rusty fell to the ground and died.

Another life lost. Only two left now.

For a while Rusty lay there, his body faint and ghostly, then he became solid again and stood up. Mefistoe was on the far side of the courtyard, waiting.

Danny moved Rusty forward and was getting ready to swing Regnum when Mefistoe threw his sword at him. It flew like an arrow and Danny flicked the control pad so that Rusty ducked. The sword skimmed over the top of his head.

Danny almost shouted out loud. He was going to win. Mefistoe didn't have a sword!

Mefistoe fell to his knees and crawled towards Rusty, begging for mercy. Rusty raised Regnum, ready to strike, but Danny hesitated – perhaps he didn't need to kill him. He could capture him and force him to set Prince free.

In a flash, Mefistoe drew a knife from his belt and stabbed it into Rusty's leg. Rusty fell to the ground and Mefistoe stabbed him again and again in the arm until he had to let go of Regnum. A moment later the knife sliced across Rusty's throat and blood spurted out. He tried to sit up but fell back and lay still.

He was dead.

Rusty's lifeline in the corner of the screen showed just one bar. One life. And then it would be GAME OVER.

Danny looked at his watch. 11.30. In less than an hour he had lost six lives.

Adam had been right – Mefistoe was evil. Evil and cunning. No wonder he had been captured by him. And no wonder Ryan had lost almost twenty fights before he had managed to finish the game.

Danny pressed PAUSE.

He put down the control pad and went to lie down on his bed. He was going to lose. He was never going to free

Prince. And Adam would never be able to cross over to the Other Side. He closed his eyes and saw his young brother, alone and scared.

Suddenly he knew that someone was in the room. He kept his eyes closed, not daring to look.

A minute went by. And another. And then he felt a small hand slip into his.

It was cold and bony. And dead.

But he folded it in his warm living hand because it was Adam's hand. And it was trembling.

He lay there, not moving, until the hand gripped him tighter. Gripped him and shook him, trying to tell him something. And Danny knew what it was. His young brother was telling him to go on. Telling him to play one more time – win or lose.

Adam's hand gave him a little squeeze and then let go.

When Danny opened his eyes, there was no one there but he knew that Adam was watching. Watching and waiting and hoping.

OK. One more game. And this time he had to win.

CHAPTER TWENTY-NINE

When he got back to the TV, Rusty was standing in the courtyard but Mefistoe was nowhere to be seen.

Good, that gave him a moment to think. Remember Ryan's advice: stay calm, take your time, see what you can use. He looked around the courtyard but there was nothing useful.

And where was Mefistoe?

Danny set off in search of him. He climbed the twisty stairs in the Dark Tower up to the first floor. He checked in all the rooms. No sign of Mefistoe. And no one on the second floor either. Was this a trap? Was Mefistoe creeping up behind him?

There was no one on the fourth floor either. Or the fifth, or the sixth, or the seventh. He reached the eighth floor and checked all the rooms. He was about to go up to the next floor when he stopped and went back to the last room he'd looked in. There was nobody there, but there was a key hanging on the wall. Maybe – just maybe …

Rusty took it off the wall and slipped it into his pocket.

Up the stairs again. Tenth floor. Eleventh. Twelfth.

And then, there on the thirteenth floor Mefistoe was

waiting, standing in front of a cell door. On the other side of the bars stood Prince.

This was it. His last chance to free him.

Rusty raised Regnum and ran at Mefistoe. The two swords clashed and the fight began. Danny used everything he had learned in his training – attack, parry, thrust. Regnum was a brilliant sword to use and he could have beaten any other enemy in an instant. But this was Mefistoe. And he was good. Very good.

Back and forth they fought – each of them looking for the moment of weakness when they could stab and kill.

Slash. Parry. Thrust.

Slash. Parry. Thrust.

And then, at last, Danny saw his opening. Mefistoe was standing near the top of the stairs. If he could just make him lose his balance …

Rusty attacked and Mefistoe moved back to avoid him. He stumbled down a step and while he was trying to get his balance, Rusty struck.

Regnum hit Mefistoe in the centre of his chest. For a moment, Danny kept the sword there, then pulled it out. Blood spread across Mefistoe's shirt and he fell forward on to his face.

Danny turned Rusty round and got the key out of his pocket. He ran to the cell door, praying that the key was the right one. He put Regnum on the floor but before he could fit the key into the lock, Prince raised his arm and pointed. Rusty spun round and Danny saw that Mefistoe was back on his feet. Blood was still running from his shirt but he had a grin on his face. He pulled his shirt open and Danny saw the trick – he was wearing body armour and a sack of fake blood.

Danny made Rusty dive to pick up Regnum but it was too late. Mefistoe charged, driving him back until he was trapped against the cell door.

Once. Twice. Three times, Mefistoe's sword jabbed into Rusty's belly.

Danny tried to keep him standing but his lifeline was flickering. Mefistoe stepped away and Rusty dropped to the ground. His body began fade until he was as transparent as a ghost.

Mefistoe was running around, jumping and laughing in his triumph.

Danny looked at the lifeline – it was flickering slower and slower but it was still there. And then he saw the key lying on the floor.

The lifeline was almost gone.

With one last effort, he moved Rusty's hand and sent the key skidding across the floor and under the cell door.

Rusty's lifeline went out.

But Prince had picked up the key. And, in a flash, he opened the door and grabbed Regnum.

Before Mefistoe knew what was happening, Prince was on to him. Danny saw Mefistoe's eyes grow wide with terror. Then Prince swung Regnum and cut off Mefistoe's head.

The hairs on the back of Danny's neck rose as a noise began in Adam's room.

For a few seconds it was just a low drumming sound but it quickly grew louder: a deep rumbling that vibrated through the floor and started to shake everything in Danny's room. He took his eyes off the screen as books began to fall off his shelf.

The noise was terrible now, booming through him, shaking his chest and making his hands tremble. The walls and floor rattled and his chair was juddering from side to side. And then a more awful sound began: cries of pain and terror. The cries turned into howling and screaming. It was if millions of people were being tortured. It filled Danny's ears, building up and up, until he felt as if it would split his head open.

And then, suddenly, it stopped and Danny slumped back in his chair.

He looked at the TV screen. Mefistoe had gone. Prince was standing there alone.

He looked amazingly, scarily, like Adam.

Prince raised his hand and then, just the way Adam used to do, he gave a cheeky grin and a thumbs-up.

The words PRINCE IS FREE flashed on to the screen.

Then the word VICTORY.

Then GAME OVER.

Then the screen went blank.

Danny turned off the console. He felt hot. He pulled off the two sweaters and threw them on the bed before he opened the door and walked out into the warm corridor. The lights were all on just as he had left them much earlier in the evening.

On his way down the stairs he peered closely at the stained glass window. The dark shadow that had looked like a monster was now simply a stain in the glass, just as the 'frightened figure' was another small flaw.

He got to the bottom step and took off Adam's basketball shirt. He looked at it and tears blurred his eyes.

He was gone. Adam was gone. He was free. Free to cross to the Other Side.

Danny sat on the step and sobbed at his loss.

And when he stopped crying, he realised that he was free too.

CHAPTER THIRTY

Danny's mobile rang while he was on the train going to Crossley Sands. He thought it must be Dad but when he looked it said UNKNOWN NUMBER.

'Is that Danny?' a woman's voice said.

'Yes.'

'You don't know me,' she went on. 'I'm Ryan's mother. I'm at the hospital. He asked me to ring you.'

'Is he OK?'

'I had a word with the doctors and they said the operation went very well. We won't be sure for a week or so, but all the signs look good.'

'Great. I'm really pleased. Say hi to him. Oh and can you tell him something else?'

'Of course. What?'

'He'll know what it means. Just tell him "Prince is free".'

The beach was deserted except for a man walking his dog in the misty distance.

Danny had only ever seen Crossley Sands in the summer when he'd been on holiday with his family, so it hardly seemed like the same place. The grey sky merged with the grey sea, and even the sand, which he remembered glowing in the sun, was drained of colour. The air was bitterly cold and it pinched his face as he, Dad and Grandad trudged down from the dunes on to the flat sand and headed for the grey concrete breakwater.

They stepped up on to the breakwater and made their way out towards the end. He and Adam used to love coming out here when they were little. It always felt as if the sea was all around them and the waves splashed over them as they shrieked and laughed. But today the sea was calm and the only movement was a slight swell, making him feel almost sick as it lifted and fell, lifted and fell, against the concrete.

'So how do we want to do this?' Dad asked.

'Emma first,' Grandad said quickly, as if he wanted to get it over with.

Danny watched, his heart knocking hard, as Dad unscrewed the lid of Mum's urn. He took the top off and looked down in the interior, shaking his head gently as if he couldn't believe what he was looking at.

'I love you, Emma. I love you,' he said, then lifted the urn and turned it upside down.

A long plume of ashes fell out, swirling away and drifting down on to the surface of the sea. Grey against grey. Danny saw them darken as they absorbed the water and began to sink. Soon all sign of Mum had disappeared.

When he took a large gasp of air, he realised that he had been holding his breath since Dad had spoken. Blood was pounding in his ears.

And now his dad began to unscrew the lid of the other urn. Danny saw him take it off and shudder as he looked inside. A shiver shook Danny, too, and his teeth began chatter.

'I can't,' Dad said, his voice cracking and his hands beginning to tremble.

'I'll do it,' Grandad said.

'No, let me,' Danny said and reached across. Dad nodded, as if it was the right thing to do and he handed the urn to him. It felt cold.

What could he say? What was the right thing to say?

The same thing Dad had said to Mum. The only thing to say – the simple truth.

'I love you, Adam,' he said.

To his amazement, he held his hand out and tipped some of the ashes into it. He closed his hand round them and felt them – a mix of soft and gritty. Of course there must be bone there too. But he wasn't shocked or disgusted. It was all that was left of Adam. But it wasn't him. He was already gone. Elsewhere.

Adam was no longer trapped in the Dark Tower. And nor was he. Winning the game had set them both free.

He opened his hand and let the ash spin away into the air and down into the sea. Then he tipped the urn and let the rest of it follow. Not Adam. Just matter. The kind Grandad had talked about, the kind that could be touched and seen and heard. But the real Adam was dark matter now. The kind that couldn't be felt or seen or heard. But which was there, invisible and everywhere.

They drove back to 13 Leylyne Road. Danny got out of the car and looked up at the house. It seemed so ordinary somehow.

'It's OK,' Dad whispered gently. 'We'll be out of this place soon. I had a text from the estate agent and they've found a house that sounds perfect. With any luck we can move in next week. Glad?'

Danny nodded, too choked to speak.

'We'll be all right,' Dad said. 'We've come through the worst. We have.'

He nodded.

'A whisky to cheer us up, Stuart?' Grandad asked.

'No – cup of tea, I think.'

Grandad smiled. 'Good idea. I'll make it.'

They watched as he went inside.

Dad put his arm round Danny's shoulder. 'They're OK. Mum and Adam,' he said. 'They're at peace. They are, you know – I really feel it. But they're still with us. By our side. And they always will be.'

'I know,' Danny said.

THE END

This Spectred Isle

Investigating Great Britain's ghosts and ghouls

By Christopher Edge

Do you believe in ghosts? Have you ever seen one? If not, then perhaps you haven't been looking in the right places. Supernatural experts who look into reports of ghostly goings-on believe that Great Britain is the most haunted country in the world. Spooky sightings have been reported at more than 10,000 different places across the country.

From screaming skulls to ghostly White Ladies, some people believe that hundreds of spine-tingling ghosts haunt our shores. However, others argue that reports of ghosts can be more easily explained. They say if you have an over-active imagination, then you are more likely to think you have seen a ghost.

Ghost hunters

Ghost hunters try and find out the truth behind reports of ghostly goings-on. Their methods include:

- studying the place where a haunting has been reported
- interviewing anyone who claims to have seen the ghost
- using hi-tech gadgets such as infra-red video cameras and digital recorders to detect any strange or unusual events.

These techniques can help ghost hunters to rule out any other explanations for the spooky events, such as ghostly figures that turn out to be tricks of the light or somebody pulling a prank. If the 'ghost' cannot be explained by natural causes, then attention can turn to more supernatural explanations. Some ghost hunters use people who claim to have psychic powers (such as the ability to see into the past or communicate with the dead) to help them.

TV programmes such as *Most Haunted* and *Paranormal Investigation: Live* show ghost hunters in action today. However, ghost hunting has been going on for many years.

The Most Haunted House in Britain

In the first half of the 20th century, a man named Harry Price became the most famous ghost hunter in Britain. He visited a Victorian mansion house in a small Essex village – Borley Rectory – which became known as the most haunted house in the country.

Built for the local vicar in 1863, Borley Rectory was soon plagued by a series of supernatural events. These included:

- doors banging shut for no reason
- objects smashing to the ground
- the sounds of strange voices, phantom footsteps and ringing bells
- mysterious writing appearing on the walls of the house the chilling apparition of a ghostly nun

- the appearance of a phantom coach driven by two
  headless horsemen through the grounds of the house.

Over the years, the families of three different vicars lived
in Borley Rectory, but each one complained about the
terrifying incidents that haunted the house. Eventually, in
1929 the Reverend Guy Smith contacted the Daily Mirror
newspaper to ask for its help. They sent Harry Price to look
into the case.

On his arrival at Borley Rectory, Price saw for himself many
of the strange events that had been reported. He saw
strange lights appear at the windows of the house when
nobody was inside, watched a candlestick fly through
the air flung by an invisible presence and even saw the
shadowy figure of the black-clad nun gliding through the
garden.

Convinced that Borley Rectory was haunted, Price decided
to investigate the case further. After yet another vicar had
moved out of the troubled house in 1937, Price moved
himself in with a team of researchers. They set about trying
to record evidence of the ghostly events.

Like a modern-day ghost hunter, Harry Price used the very
latest equipment available. He set up cameras and installed
telephones so he could talk to his researchers wherever
they were in the house. During the year that he stayed at
the rectory, no ghosts were captured on camera, but Price

claimed to have contacted two ghostly spirits from beyond the grave.

He said that one of the spirits was the ghost of a nun who had been murdered at Borley in 1667. Her remains were buried beneath the rectory; that was the reason that her ghost couldn't rest. Price's second ghostly encounter was an even more frightening one. He said that he had contacted a vengeful spirit named Sunex Amures. This ghost announced that it was going to burn Borley Rectory to the ground.

After a year of ghost hunting, Price finally moved out of the rectory. Many people believed that he had made up his stories of ghostly events in order to become famous. However, eleven months after Price had left Borley Rectory, the house burned down in a mysterious fire. When the cellar of the ruined rectory was dug out, the remains of a skeleton were discovered. Could Harry Price really have received a message from beyond the grave?

Around Great Britain in eighty ghosts

Although Borley Rectory burned to the ground, there are many more haunted houses where ghosts are said to prowl. Would you be brave enough to visit any of the following places after dark?

- Arundel Castle in West Sussex is haunted by the ghost of a young woman dressed in white. The White Lady wanders the castle on moonlit nights.
- The ghost of an eighteenth century actor haunts the Theatre Royal in London's Drury Lane. Wearing a long grey

coat, a three-cornered hat and a powdered wig, the ghost watches the plays from the balcony. Many people believe that if the ghost appears the play will be a hit!

- Ghosts of soldiers from the English Civil War are believed to haunt Littledean Hall in Gloucestershire. Visitors have reported seeing a phantom bloodstain appear on the floor of the dining room. This marks the spot where two Royalist soldiers were murdered by a Roundhead spy.

- Finally, Charlton House in Greenwich, London is haunted by a more unusual breed of ghost. A plague of phantom rabbits are said to roam the third floor of the building! These rabbits are said to be the ghosts of the bunnies who were kept there during the Second World War.

Haunted highways

Where do you think the most haunted road in Great Britain is? A dark, spooky lane beside the ruins of a church? An old straight track in the middle of an ancient forest? How about one of the longest and busiest roads in the country – the M6 motorway? This 230-mile stretch of tarmac has had more supernatural sightings than any other road in Britain. Frightened drivers have reported seeing ghostly legions of Roman soliders marching down the highway, phantom hitchhikers thumbing a ride and spectral lorries appearing out of the mist.

We would like to thank the following schools and students for all their help in developing and trialling *Ghost Game*.

Queensbridge School, Birmingham

Farhan Akmal, Farees Almatari, Junaid Asif, Chloe Bartlett, Shane Bevan, Tyler Blair-Thompson, Shahid Farooq, Danial Hussain, Umayr Hussain, Arbaz Mohammed Khan, Kadeem Khan, Umer Khan, Ihtishaam Majid, Arslan Mehmood, Sophie Pinnegar, Aaron Reatus, Jamie-Lee Smith, Roche Smith, Abdalla Suleiman, Imran Uddin, Saqib Ul-Hassan, Chulothe Urooj, Keiran Von-Breen, Nikolas Watkins, Oliver Watkins, Grace Williams, Raakib Zaman

Acle High School, Norwich

Mustafa Afsar, Mohammed Akmal Ali, Nassar Ayaz, Azharudeen Basheer Ahmed, Andre Christian, Jordan Easie, Antoinette Grant, Kia Greaves, Conor Handel, Waseem Hanif, Kabeer Javed, Zeshan Javed, Abel Johnson, Selina King, Ismaeel Muhammed Majid, Aziz Rehman, Abdul Wahid